CHUNKS OF TERROR
VOL. 1

By
Steve Hudgins

Copyright © 2023 Steve Hudgins
All rights reserved

This is a work of fiction.
Names, characters, places and incidents either are the products of the author's imagination or are used fictitiously.
Any resemblance to actual persons, living or dead, businesses, companies, events, or locales is entirely coincidental.

A QUICK WORD FROM THE AUTHOR

They say I'm crazy.
Just a little bit out of whack.
Lock your doors and bolt your windows.
I'm clearly a maniac.

It's me, your friendly neighborhood Maniac on the Loose!

Welcome to Vol. 1 of my latest horror anthology series, *Chunks of Terror.*

Inside you will find over 20 terrifying tales told in a "true story" style that will curdle your blood and send shivers down your spine!

Before we embark on our dark journey, I do want make sure you are aware of my website:
www.maniacontheloose.com
There you will find information on all of my books, audiobooks and my scary stories podcast.
Anyone who signs up for my free newsletter while they're there will get instant access to some free stuff!

Now it's time for *Chunks of Terror Vol. 1.*

Keep your arms and legs inside the vehicle at all times and enjoy the ride.

THE MOONRISE MANOR HOTEL

Near Lookout Valley Tennessee is a towering stone structure that was erected in 1889. It was originally a hospital called Moonrise Institution. The hospital eventually became infamous for its unethical medical experiments on patients that many considered to be nothing short of torture.

After countless patients died ghastly deaths, the hospital was condemned and permanently closed their doors in 1909.

Six years after the closing of the Moonrise Institution, a young entrepreneur named Jacob Manor purchased the hospital and its surrounding grounds. He had a dream of turning the impressive building into a luxury hotel.

During the extensive renovations it took to transform the drab hospital into the magnificent, vast five story hotel it is today, many of the builders reported having unusual experiences.

Many of the men described seeing shadowy figures roaming the halls. Tools were reported missing daily.

Numerous incidents involving extension ladders falling resulted in multiple deaths. Some workers felt as though there was something within the building that didn't want them there.

During the hotel's opening night, a man named Phillip Belvidere fell down The Moonshine Manor Hotel's grand staircase and later succumbed to his injuries. Before he passed, Mr. Belvidere told doctors that someone shoved him from behind. However, all of the witnesses to the fall noted that there were no people near Mr. Belvidere when he tumbled down the staircase.

That was just the beginning of a long string of paranormal encounters that continue to this day.

It's not uncommon for anyone who stays at The Moonrise Manor Hotel to experience some form of paranormal activity. Most of the encounters are benign in nature. However, many people have had darker experiences.

The following are some of the more chilling tales to come from those who have visited The Moonrise Manor Hotel.

ROOM 212

The Moonrise Manor Hotel is a resort hotel. Most people go there for vacations. I, on the other hand, was traveling and needed a place to stay for the night. It was the only hotel I could find with a vacancy.

I remember when I was checking in how cozy the hotel felt. The lobby walls were a warm, dark red color. The busy carpet patterns were a mix of red and gold. I was thinking that it would be a nice place to visit when I had more time. Later that night, I changed my mind about that.

I was tired from driving and had no trouble falling asleep. I woke up in the middle of the night. The room was dark, but I was still able to notice movement in the corner of the room.

I focused my eyes on that area and noticed a strange orange light. It would occasionally get brighter and then grow dimmer, but it was always there.

As my eyes adjusted to the darkness, I could ever so slightly make out a figure. It appeared to be a woman with long, scraggly hair sitting in a chair in the corner of the room. The orange light was flickering in front of her face. That's when I realized what the light was.

It was the tip of a lit cigarette. The scent of stale smoke in the air confirmed what I was seeing. There was a woman sitting in my room smoking a cigarette!

I quickly turned on the lamp next to the bed and found myself staring at an empty chair. There was no woman in it. There was no cigarette and the smoke smell had disappeared as well.

I convinced myself it was a dream of some kind and went back to sleep. I was awakened later that night by the sound of a wheezing cough. The stench of cigarette smoke was drifting through the air once more. When I opened my eyes, I saw the silhouette and the orange tip of the cigarette glowing bright as the woman took in a hefty puff.

I turned the light on and again. The woman and the smell of cigarettes were gone.

I thought about asking to switch rooms, but I was so tired, I decided to just go back to sleep. I had no further incidents and checked out early the next morning.

THE 3RD FLOOR HALLWAY

The Moonrise Manor Hotel has the reputation of being haunted. After staying three nights in the hotel, my husband and I hadn't experienced anything unusual at all.

On our fourth day, we had taken in some of the sights around town and had a late dinner in the hotel. My husband was tired and went to the room to turn in while I spent some time in the hotel's gift shop.

After purchasing a few gifts for friends, I headed back to our room on the 3rd floor. As I turned the corner, I spotted a young boy sitting in the middle of the cornflower blue hallway. He was bouncing a ball against a wall.

The boy couldn't have been more than 6 years old. And his attire was out of date. He was wearing clothes that looked like they were from the 1920's era. He was cute as a button. He had chubby cheeks and the brightest blue eyes.

When the young boy spotted me he stood up at attention as if he were caught doing something he wasn't supposed to be doing.

I smiled at the boy.

"Hello there, what's your name?"

He watched me for a moment before he spoke up.

"William. But I'm not supposed to talk to strangers."

With that, he turned and walked down the hall and around the corner.

I guess it was the motherly instinct within me that compelled me to follow the boy to make sure he made it back to his room without incident.

When I reached the end of the 3rd floor hallway and rounded the corner, I spotted the boy. He was standing at the top of the staircase staring at me. Once he saw me he hurried down the stairs.

I followed him. Every once in a while the boy would stop and look at me. It was as though he were waiting for me to catch up with him.

I followed him to the 1st floor lobby and felt concerned when he dashed through the back door and outside.

"Where are you going?"

I was worried about the little boy being outside that late at night by himself. I picked up my pace, exited the hotel and made my way down a thin cobblestone path until I saw the boy again. He was standing in the hotel cemetery.

I had taken one of the hotel's ghost tours a couple nights back and they explained that back in the old days, if hotel guests died and there was no family to claim the body, they'd simply bury them in the hotel cemetery.

"You shouldn't be playing outside at night all alone. You could get lost. You could get hurt."

The boy was standing in front of an old, faded headstone. His face held no expression. He stood statuesque until I realized that he was dissipating into the air and suddenly, he was just gone.

I don't know how long I stood standing in confusion before I walked forward to the headstone the little boy had been standing in front of.

The headstone read:
William Tucker
Born 1923
Died 1929

ROOM 425

When I was 18 years old, I was visiting a college in the Lookout Valley. It was the first time I ever traveled alone. My father wasn't thrilled about it, but I explained to him that if I was going away to college, I was going to have to get used to traveling alone and it would be a good experience for me. He reluctantly agreed.

I was blown away by The Moonrise Manor Hotel! It was huge and old. I had never seen a stone building that big before. It gave me castle vibes. If I had known that it was supposed to be haunted, I probably wouldn't have stayed there because ghost stuff creeps me out. But I didn't know. I just picked it because it was near where I was going and it had good reviews.

My college visit went great. I had all but decided that was the college for me. The excitement of visiting the campus and getting closer to the next chapter of my life had me worn down by the end of the day and I went to bed early.

I'm the kind of person who sleeps like the dead. Once my head hits a pillow, I'm out until morning unless someone makes a point to wake me up. And that's exactly what happened.

I was in a deep sleep. I was dreaming of swimming in a river, but during the swim, a gigantic snake wrapped itself around my thigh and was slithering up and down it.

I woke up with a gasp and was relieved once I realized it was just a dream. However, I could still feel the snake sliding up and down my leg!

When I looked down, I saw a man sitting on the foot of my bed. The room was dark, so I couldn't see him well. What I could see was that he was an older man in his 50's or 60's. He was balding and wearing a hospital gown of some sort. And he was breathing heavy. In an excited, sexual kind of way.

That's when I realized that he was running his hand up and down my thigh.

I screamed as loud as I could, jumped from the bed and turned on the light, but the man was no longer there.

I assumed he had bolted out of the room once I woke up, so I chased after him. I wasn't going to let that pervert get away with what he did. I was going to point him out to the hotel staff and have them call the cops on the creep.

When I rushed out into the hallway, there was nobody there. I looked both ways and saw no one.

My room was in the middle of the floor. If he had run out into the hallway, I would have seen him. So, where did he go?

That's when I felt hot breath on the back of my neck and then felt a hand firmly grasp my behind.

I spun around with a shriek and couldn't believe that there was nobody there! Then my hotel room door slammed shut.

I screamed and screamed until other hotel attendees and staff rushed to my aid. I told them all what happened. The hotel manager unlocked my room and the staff did a thorough search, but there was nobody in the room.

I left the hotel that night and decided to go to college in a state far away from there.

ROOM 436

When I was in my early 20's my sister and I took a short vacation to The Moonrise Manor Hotel, specifically because it was haunted!

We were hoping for some paranormal action and asked the front desk clerk to put us in the most haunted room they had available. He said that the 4th floor tended to be the area where most people got terrified. He even warned us that young women were particularly prone to disturbing encounters on the 4th floor. He explained that back when the building was a hospital, a crazy doctor did his most sinister experiments on that floor. He said the patients who died may have been the lucky ones because some of them turned into bloodthirsty maniacs.

After hearing all of that, I was a little bit reluctant, but my sister was all for it, so he put us in room 436.

It was our first night there. My sister had already gotten dressed and wanted to explore the hotel a little before our dinner reservations. While my sister was able to get ready in a flash, I took some time. I still had to shower and put my make up on, so as not to disappoint her, I told her to explore without me and

I'd just meet her at the hotel restaurant and she agreed.

As soon as my sister left, the entire room got cold. I couldn't figure out why, but it wasn't cold enough to keep me from my shower, so I got to it.

The hot water against my skin was refreshing and I was in the process of wetting my hair when the shower curtain was jerked open. I let out a startled squeal, expecting to see someone standing there, but there wasn't.

The bathroom was small and the door was shut. Nobody could have opened the shower curtain and gotten out of the bathroom without me seeing them, but I was alone.

There was no logical explanation for what happened. The curtain was pulled open in a way that could not have happened on its own.

I stood there dumbfounded thinking it all through when I felt someone grab the back of my hair and yank my head back. I was then viciously shoved against the white, tiled shower wall.

I fought back against my attacker, but there was nobody there. It was just me in the shower. Still, I could feel a large man's muscular body pinning me against the wall while his catcher's mitt-like hand began exploring my body. I was hollering at the top of my lungs as I felt the ghostly hand slide down my stomach to my vagina.

I was crying out when I heard someone break down my hotel door and then burst into the bathroom. The invisible force was continuing to assault me until two men reached me and pulled me out of the shower.

The two men who rescued me had heard my screams as they walked down the hall. They said once they got into the bathroom, all they saw was me plastered against the wall. They didn't see anybody else.

Mentally, I never fully recovered from that incident. Some people don't believe me. They think I made the whole thing up, but I didn't. And I'm not crazy.

That really happened.

THE FRONT DESK

I'm a paranormal fiction writer and I like to stay at locations that have a haunted history for ideas and inspiration.

I booked a weeklong stay at The Moonrise Manor Hotel. The hotel was immense and beautiful. It was clearly an ancient hotel. This was evident by its stone exterior and the vintage aura of the décor.

I was getting a few ideas, but with as much buzz as there was about the hotel being haunted, I guess I was expecting more. For the most part, it was just an old hotel.

I usually don't go to bed before 3:00am. I decided to stroll through the hotel at 2:00am. I figured there wouldn't be anyone else around at that time and the atmosphere would be different and I was correct. Walking through the hotel's long corridors alone, without being distracted by the stirring of others, definitely amped up the creepy factor.

When I found myself in the lobby I was slightly startled by the voice of the front desk clerk.

"You're up late."

I turned to see a young man in a bellhop uniform standing behind the front desk. He was in his early 20's and had sandy blonde hair that was parted sharply on the side. He was very professional in appearance.

"I'm a night owl."

The clerk nodded.

"We have that in common."

I walked up to the front desk and got comfortable as I casually leaned on the counter.

"So, as an employee here, have you experienced anything paranormal?"

He was quick to answer.

"I was outside sweeping the porch area when I saw a woman standing at the other end of the porch. She was dressed in clothing from a different period and was cradling firewood. She never acknowledged me. Her mind was elsewhere. Then she turned and walked into the storage closet. Now, the storage closet doesn't lead anywhere. It's just a closet. I thought it odd that she was taking firewood into it, so I entered the closet and there was nobody there."

"A ghost?"

He shrugged.

"I don't have the answers. I can only tell you what I experienced."

The front desk clerk studied my face for a moment before he discreetly peered about the lobby.

"That's nothing though. You want to see something really scary?"

I was game.

"Absolutely."

The young front desk clerk led me to the end of the building and opened a wooden door that led to a narrow areaway.

"When they were remodeling the building they added an extra section to house the staff back in the old days. This thin areaway is the passage between the original building and newer section."

He then pointed up.

"Do you see those wood beams?"

There were two thick wooden beams near the top of the areaway.

"Perfect for someone to hang themselves from."

The front desk clerk's voice had taken on a sinister tone when he spoke that sentence. I turned and looked at him. His eyes were glistening and he held a false smile that sent chills down my spine. He said not another word. He simply stared at me.

"Are you okay? You're acting strange."

The young man didn't respond by speaking. He held his maniacal gaze on me as he pointed to the beams.

As I looked up, a flash of lighting lit the areaway and I saw the swaying body of a young man with a noose around his neck hanging from the wooden beam. Upon closer look, it was the front desk clerk.

I spun around to see if he was still standing in the areaway with me, but he was not. I looked back up at the beam and the body was no longer there either.

I hurried out of the areaway and rushed to the front desk to confront the young man. I wasn't sure what kind of game he was playing, but his trick scared the hell out of me and I was fuming.

When I got to the front desk, I was greeted by a white haired man in his 70's.

"Have you seen the other front desk clerk?"

The older man seemed confused.

"Other front desk clerk?"

"The young man in the bellhop outfit. Blonde hair parted on the side. Early twenties."

"I'm sorry sir, but there's nobody that works for the hotel who fits that description."

That couldn't be. Obviously the old man was mistaken.

"I was just talking to him!"

"I'm the only desk clerk on duty until eight in the morning."

I shook my head and became animated as I spoke.

"He took me into the areaway and tried to scare me by showing me a dead body dangling from the beams."

The front desk clerk became white as a ghost as he looked back and forth between me and the area I spoke of. Obviously something was wrong.

"What? What is it?"

I could see his mind trying to put something together and finally he explained.

"I'm confused. You see, the areaway you spoke of doesn't exist anymore. It was taken down in the 1950's after a bellhop hung himself in there."

THE LONG WAY HOME

I was driving home from college during fall break. It was normally a two hour drive, but being that I'm the kind of girl who loves the changing of seasons, I decided to extend my ride home by driving deep into the woods with the hopes of seeing some brilliant fall colors.

It was a direction that added nearly forty minutes of travel time to my ride home. I had taken the route in question a couple times before when I was feeling adventurous and was in an extended driving mood, but had never experienced it during autumn.

My hunch of what beauty it may behold during peak foliage time was correct. The woods had erupted into an explosion of gold, amber, crimson and rust! It was nothing short of magnificent.

My eyes were so locked onto the beauty of the trees that I barely saw the gigantic buck jump out in front of my car. I stomped on the brakes and came to a screeching halt just inches from the impressive creature's muscled body.

The buck stood relaxed, never having flinched by the near collision. It stared directly at me for a brief moment as if offended by my presence before finally prancing away.

I let out a deep breath and stepped on the accelerator to get moving again, only to realize that my car had died. A chill ran through my body. This was not the ideal place to have a breakdown.

A wave of relief splashed over me when I turned the key and the engine roared to life. Unfortunately, my comfort was premature as the car died out again as soon as I shifted it into drive. I repeated the process over a dozen times before I came to the realization that I wasn't going to be able to drive my car.

I immediately pulled out my cellphone and wouldn't you know it, there was no cell service. I was stranded all alone in the middle of nowhere.

I sat in my car for twenty minutes in hopes that someone would stop and help me, but not a single car drove by, so I decided to get out and start walking.

The nearest town was a thirty minute drive away, so I realized there was no way I was making it there any time soon on foot. My hope was that somewhere down the road, I'd get cell service and could call for help.

An hour later I still hadn't found a cell signal and not one car had passed by. To top it off, a mist of rain was starting up.

I was in real trouble.

I grew optimistic when I heard the distant hum of an engine and it was getting closer! Someone was coming down the road!

As the vehicle came into view, I recognized it as an extremely old, flat bed pickup truck. It was rusted to hell. The truck slowed and came to a halt next to me. The driver leaned over and unrolled the passenger's side window.

"Hey baby. What's a little fox like you doin' all alone out this way?"

The man was slender and had long greasy hair. He was wearing a filthy white tank top covered with a thin camouflage jacket.

"Um, my car broke down."

He nodded and flashed a tobacco stained smile.

"Yeah, I saw it."

I felt extremely uncomfortable as the dirty man looked me up and down for an inappropriate amount of time before continuing.

"Hop on in, I'll give you a lift to town."

I looked the truck over as I considered his offer. That's when I saw that he had a bloody deer carcass lying on the flatbed of his truck. He noticed that I was eyeing the animal.

"Oh don't worry about her. She won't bite. Get on in here."

He pushed the driver's side door open.

I stood still as I contemplated my options which were basically accepting his ride or continuing to walk on my own. I could see the impatience in his face as he waited for me. I didn't want to keep him waiting any longer.

"Thank you, but I think I'll just walk."

He chuckled.

"Walk? Walk to where? The nearest town is a thirty minute drive from here. It'll take you eight hours to walk there. Now stop being a damn fool and get in this truck."

It was then that the mist of rain transitioning into a heavy drizzle made me change my mind and I reluctantly got into the strange man's truck which reeked of body odor and stale tobacco water.

"Glad to see you came to your senses."

With that he started driving. For the next several minutes he didn't say anything else. He just kept glancing at me and staring down in the region of my breasts. When he realized I was aware of what he was doing, he spoke up.

"I like your jacket, there."

My jacket that he was pretending to admire so much was a simple, tan windbreaker. I figured since I caught him, he'd at least be more discreet with his gawking, but that wasn't the case.

"Yeah, I like that jacket a lot. I like them pants too."

I played dumb and tried to remain polite until he got me to town. At any given time he could opt to pull over and kick me out. Or worse.

"Thank you."

My general uneasiness grew into full blown fear when he turned off of the main road and onto a dirt path.

"Hey! Where are you going? Why are you turning here?"

"Relax sugar britches. I'm stopping at my homestead. I gotta dump off the deer. Then I'll take you to town."

"You can just drop me off here."

He laughed as he spit a wad of tobacco juice onto the truck floor and wiped his mouth off with the back of his hand.

"Settle down girly, we're almost there."

It was just a few seconds later when we arrived at the grimy man's home. It was a literal shack that appeared to be slapped together with various shapes of scrap wood planks. The large rusty metal pipe that was sticking out of the middle of the hut was spewing out smoke. But it wasn't the house that caught my eye immediately. It was the surrounding trees that had dozens of deer carcasses hanging from thick branches. He spoke up when he heard me gasp at the gruesome sight.

"I only eat deer meat."

That's when I noticed the stockpile of junked cars littering his land. From ancient and rusty to brand new, he had hundreds of vehicles scattered about as far as the eye could see.

When he pulled to a stop, he gave me a smile and wink.

"Whaddya say little girl? Want to come in and have a hot cup of coffee and some deviled eggs? I made 'em myself."

I immediately shook my head.

"No. No, thank you. I'm just going to wait here for you."

"Suit yourself."

The man shut the engine of the old truck off, withdrew his keys and got out of the vehicle. As he began pulling the deer carcass off the back of his flatbed, I realized this rather terrifying situation may have been a blessing in disguise! I quickly rolled down my window and hollered out to him."

"Hey, do you have a phone in your house I can use?"

"No phone."

I deflated and sulked as I watched the man pull the deer body around the back of his house and out of sight.

I wasn't sure what to do. I had an urge to get out of the truck and run away. On the other hand, with the exception of ogling me and being a bit creepy, he hadn't hurt me in any way. If he meant me harm that likely would have already happened. So I waited for him.

As I waited, I pulled out my phone on the off chance that somehow there would be a cell signal even deeper in the woods and not surprisingly, there wasn't. What was surprising however was the fact that my cellphone was informing me that there was a Wi-Fi signal available in the area. I immediately tried to connect my phone to it, but it was protected by a password.

How was there a Wi-Fi signal out there? That's what I was thinking when I noticed the satellite dish on the edge of the man's shack.

Did he have internet service? If he did, surely he had a phone. And if he had a phone, why did he tell me he didn't?

This wasn't good. I again, contemplated whether or not to run away, but instead, I felt compelled to get closer to his house to see if he had a phone. If he did and I could reach it, I could call 911. That would at least alert someone of my predicament. As it was, I was at the mercy of the strange man who had me feeling uneasy to say the least.

I got out of the car. The stench of rotting deer was haunting the air around me as I slowly approached the man's house. As I got closer I could hear the man inside the shack talking to someone.

When I reached a window, I pushed my face close to the pane of grimy glass and peered into his ransacked house. I was looking into the small kitchen area which was cluttered with old, empty, food cans and dirty dishes. I saw the man's truck keys lying on the kitchen table amongst a collection of disorder.

I instinctively ducked down when I saw the man come into view. When I popped my head back up I could see him pacing back and forth as he talked on a phone. He was close enough that I could hear him clearly.

"…tow her car out here and we'll put it with the rest of them. I'd say she's in her early 20's. Blonde hair. Hot little body. We'll definitely have some fun with her tonight…"

I jumped and screamed when I heard the savage barking of a dog directly behind me. I turned to see a black German shepherd. His snarl was ferocious and his barking was relentless. Slobber began dripping from his mouth as if he were eyeing me as his dinner.

"Get over here, dog!"

The dog obeyed his master and ran behind the man who was standing and staring at me with evil intent glistening in his eyes.

"What are you doing over there?"

I spit out the first thing that popped into my mind that I thought the man might believe.

"Do you have a bathroom I could use?"

He flashed his tobacco stained smile as he pointed around in all directions.

"The world is one big toilet. Pick a spot, darlin'."

I smiled, nodded and took that opportunity to duck behind the house.

Based on what I heard the man say on the phone, it was clear that he and his friend had sick plans that included me. I feared I wouldn't survive the night. If I was going to get away, I had to come up with a plan now before he got suspicious. I could just run off into the woods, but that likely wouldn't bode well for me. Besides, his beast of a dog would easily run me down.

That's when I remembered the keys on his kitchen table. If I could sneak into the house and get his keys, maybe I could get to the truck and escape!

I found a rickety back door to his house that wasn't even latched. It creaked slightly as I opened it, but not enough for the man to hear. I immediately saw the kitchen table in the far room and was relieved to see the keys still sitting on them. But my attention was quickly drawn to the room I was standing in.

The walls of the room were wallpapered with pinups of nude women in the raunchiest of poses. There was a huge wooden table in the center of the room that had leather restraints on the top and bottom as if for wrists and ankles. At the far end of the table was a video camera sitting atop a tripod.

The plans they had for me were no longer a mystery. This was officially a life or death situation!

I hurried into the kitchen and just as I grabbed the keys from the table, I heard the man's voice.

"Caught ya' red handed."

I looked up and saw the man standing in the doorway holding the most devious of grins.

I had to make a choice and fast. I opted for aggression and charged the man. His eyes widened in shock as I rushed toward him. He clearly wasn't expecting that tactic. I reached him before he could properly react and I shoved him with all of my strength which sent him crashing to the floor.

As I bolted from the house and raced toward the truck, I heard the man yell out "Get her, dog! Get her!"

The savage dog dashed toward me in a blur. I was close to the truck when the dog clasped onto the bottom of my pant leg and began pulling me. As I fell to the ground and felt myself being dragged back toward the shack, I saw the man stroll out of the house confidently.

"You ain't goin' nowhere ya' little bitch! We're gonna have us a sex party tonight and you're the guest of honor!"

As soon as that disgusting statement exited his mouth, the bottom of my pants leg ripped off into the dog's mouth freeing me momentarily. I jumped up, threw myself into the truck and slammed the door shut just as the vicious dog leapt up onto the hood, barking ferociously.

I looked up as I fumbled with the keys and saw the man running toward the truck. I quickly locked the doors, but that didn't stop him from pounding on the windows. The passenger's side window shattered from his blows as I turned the key and started the engine.

I looked down at the stick shift. I hadn't driven a stick in years, so I was going to be rusty. Just as the man attempted to climb in through the window to grab me, I grinded the gear into reverse and spun the truck around. The force of the turn threw the man to the ground. I shoved the stick shift into first gear and peeled down the driveway. By the time I slammed it into second gear, there was no catching me.

As I drove away and left the demented man and his dungeon of doom in the dust, I found myself giving thanks to my father for insisting that I learn how to drive a stick shift when I was younger.

THE NERVOUS BARTENDER

I'm a bartender for a little hole in the wall bar called the Golden Bullet. It's located in the historic district of a small town. We're open Monday through Saturday from 11am to 3am.

On Friday and Saturday nights the bar is packed all the way until closing time, but Monday through Thursday, most customers vacate the premises by 11:00pm.

I asked the owner why he insisted on staying open until 3:00am during the week. He simply stated that it had always been that way and it always will.

I was a single guy who lived alone, so I didn't have anyone waiting for me. And the bar had a nice TV. After tidying things up and doing inventory, I'd just sit on my ass and watch movies until 3:00am. If the boss wanted to pay me to do that, who was I to complain?

It was a Wednesday night, one of the slowest nights of the week and it was getting close to 2:00am. The last paying customer left at approximately 11:00pm. A local wino came in to take a leak in the bathroom at around midnight. We weren't supposed to let him do that, but as long as the owner wasn't around to chew me out, I didn't see the harm in it. Otherwise, it was quiet. Hell, I hadn't even seen a car drive past in over an hour.

I was watching an old episode of *The Love Boat* on TV when the door to the bar was flung open and a woman rushed inside. She appeared to be in her late 30's. She had long blonde hair that was messed up and she had a deep bruise around one of her eyes. The frantic woman rushed up to the bar and latched onto the front of my shirt.

"Help me! You have to help me!"

"What is it lady? What's wrong?"

"There's a crazy woman after me! She's going to kill me!"

I reached for my phone under the bar.

"I'll call the police!"

The panicked woman pushed the phone from my hand.

"No! You can't call the police!"

She pulled me closer to her.

"They're in on it!"

"In on it? In on what?"

"There's no time! You have to hide me! She's coming! She'll kill me!"

"There's no place to hide you. This is just a little bar…"

"The bathroom. Where's the bathroom?"

I pointed toward the darkened far end of the bar.

"Back there."

"I'm going to hide in the bathroom. A crazy woman is going to come in here looking for me. Tell her you haven't seen me!"

As the hysterical woman turned to bolt toward the bathroom, I grabbed her by the shirt and halted her.

"I can't do this. You don't understand. When I get nervous, I stutter and ramble and…I'm…I'm...afraid I'll give you away!"

Her face wrinkled with concern.

"My life depends on you!"

"Oh boy, you don't want to put your life in my hands. I'm…I'm not good at lying. I can never play poker. Everyone knows the instant I have a good hand. I'm…I'm…I'm afraid I'll get you killed!

She pulled free from my grip.

"Please! Don't tell her I'm here!"

I watched on as the hyper woman scrambled to the back of the bar and disappeared into the bathroom.

Within seconds of the bathroom door closing shut, I heard the clinking of the bar's front door opening. My eyes opened wide at the intimidating figure darkening the Golden Bullet's doorway. She was a tall, muscular woman in her early 40's. She had a long, ghastly permanent scar running along the right side of her jawline. She was leather clad and had straight, fiery red hair. One of her boots had a spur that jingled with every step she took. I gulped as she walked toward the bar.

"Uh…hi. Can I uh…can I help you?"

The menacing woman stepped to the bar and glared at me with her dark, mean eyes. She didn't say a word. She held that sharp gaze on me as she withdrew a cigarette from a soft pack.

"Uh…there's…there's…not supposed to be any smoking in here…"

The woman wasn't fazed by my feeble words as she struck a match and lit her cigarette with the flame.

"But…yeah, it's okay if you want to smoke. I mean…there's nobody else here…it's just you and me. Nobody else at all. I mean…nobody has been here all night, practically. No woman came here recently or anything like that. Nope. It's just you and me. So yeah, go ahead and smoke. I don't mind. Since there's nobody else here. Yeah, I don't mind…I don't mind at all…so yeah…that's fine."

The scary woman continued to stare through me. I didn't have the guts to hold eye contact with her. My gaze sheepishly sloped to her neck and focused on the skull and crossbones tattoo which had the words "Dead Men Tell No Tales" stenciled underneath it.

As the woman exhaled a cloud of smoke, I glanced up and could see her eyebrows furrow as she examined me. Her voice was as rough as expected.

"What the hell are you so nervous about?"

Sweat began pouring down my face.

"Nervous? I'm not nervous? I'm calm as a cucumber. I'm not nervous at all…I mean…why…why…why would you think I'm nervous?"

The terrifying woman smiled revealing a chipped front tooth.

"She's here, isn't she?"

I shook my head vigorously as I stammered.

"Nope. She's not here. Nobody's here. Just me. And you, of course. I mean…yeah, of course you're here. As if you didn't know *you* were here. Of course you knew. I mean…yeah…so if by, *she* you meant *you*…well then yeah, in that case she's here…but otherwise, no. She's not here. There's nobody else here.

The scary woman moved her face in closer to me and whispered sharply.

"Where is she?"

At that point sweat was dripping from my face and onto the bar and my heart was fluttering with fear. My nervous energy was out of control as was my stammering madness.

"I don't know where she is. I mean…if she were here, I wouldn't know where she is. But she's not here. So…yeah…does that answer your question?"

My eyes began to inadvertently dart back and forth from the intimidating woman to the bathroom where the victim was hiding. The chilling woman's eyes followed mine and froze on the bathroom door. She slowly turned her face back to mine and her smile grew larger as she pulled a gigantic revolver out from under her leather jacket.

As the woman stepped away from the bar and began cautiously moving toward the bathroom, I said everything I could to dissuade her.

"Whoever you're looking for is not in the bathroom. I can tell you that much. If someone came in here and was looking to hide, the last place they'd be is the bathroom. So…so…so yeah, you don't even have to look there. There's definitely nobody in the bathroom!"

The beastly woman had completely tuned me out as she inched toward the bathroom door. I had to assume she was going to open the bathroom door and blast the poor victim to oblivion.

It was my fault that the poor woman was about to be killed. If I were a cool customer and not such a nervous, blabbering fool, I could have probably saved her. Instead, I was going to be the reason she was murdered and I wasn't sure I could live with that. I had to do something to help that poor woman.

As the intimidating, red haired killer reached out to grab the bathroom doorknob I raced up behind her and smashed a whiskey bottle over her head. That sent the big woman crashing to the floor with a thud.

I looked down at the scary woman. She was dazed, but not completely out cold. This woman was tough! I had to hurry!

I opened the bathroom door to find the poor pitiful, bruised woman curled up in a defensive ball against the wall. I quickly motioned to her.

"The coast is clear! Run!"

The woman appeared confused for a few seconds until she saw the hulking brute lying on the floor. A smile covered her face as she jumped up, grabbed me, gave me a hard hug and then looked deeply into my eyes as she spoke sincerely.

"Thank you. You saved my life. Thank you so much."

We stared at each other for another second before she rushed out of the bar.

I looked down at the disoriented red head. I didn't know how long it would be before her cobwebs would clear so I hurried back to the bar, picked up my phone and called the police.

As soon as I hung up with the police and looked up from my phone, I startled. The intimidating red head was standing in front of the bar glaring at me menacingly.

I thought I was a goner. I started mumbling as I searched for words that may persuade the evil woman from killing me.

"Please...I, uh…don't…uh…please…"

The frightening woman took in a deep breath and then expelled it. As she exhaled her expression slowly transitioned from rage to disappointment. She then plopped down onto one of the bar stools.

"Give me a beer."

I didn't hesitate to do as she ordered.

"Uh…just so you know, I called the police so…uh…yeah, if you're thinking of killing me…uh…you'll probably get caught if you do…so maybe you don't want to kill me, then? I mean…it might not be a good idea with the cops coming and all."

The big red head took a long swig of the beer and then placed the cold bottle on the large knot atop her head.

"That woman you just saved is Margaret Moss. Ever hear of her?"

I shook my head.

"You may know her better as Margaret the Monster. The serial killer who kidnaps kids, kills them, chops off their hands and mails them to their parents."

My heart sank.

"And you are…?"

"A bounty hunter."

The redheaded bounty hunter finished the rest of the beer in one gulp and gave me one last cold glare before exiting the Golden Bullet.

I wish I could say that the bounty hunter or the police caught up with Margaret the Monster later that night, but they didn't. I know that because a week later the news reported that Margaret the Monster had claimed yet another child victim.

THE FOUR IMAGES

A trail camera is a battery operated weatherproof camera that can be placed in remote areas and will automatically snap photos when motion is sensed in front of the camera.

I live in the deep woods. It's such an isolated, quiet location that no humans come anywhere near this neck of the woods except during hunting season.

I own over one hundred acres. Most of it woodland. There's a long walking trail that snakes through the majority of the forest on my land. It ends at an open section of field. That's where I place my trail camera. I tie it to a tree at the forest's edge and point it in the direction of the clearing.

I'm not a hunter. I use the trail camera because I like being aware of the animals in the region. There's entertainment value as well. I enjoy looking at candid photos of the wild animals in their natural environment. I retrieve my trail camera every three days and go through all the pictures taken in that time span.

Some of my favorite images that have been captured by the trail camera over the years include two young bucks locking horns, the entire clearing filled with crows, a rare bobcat, a huge doe in mid-leap, a great owl clutching a mouse, a family of foxes napping and an albino turkey.

The most alarming images were taken three months ago. There were four images in total. They were all taken between 1:00am and 1:30am.

IMAGE 1
1:02am

At first, I didn't notice anything unusual. It was simply an image of the empty field. I assumed a wind gust moved some tall grass around enough to trigger the motion sensor.

Then I saw it.

At the far end of the clearing appeared to be a solid object. It was difficult to make out in detail as it was shrouded in darkness, but I could clearly see the outline of it. It appeared to be saucer shaped and it was large. I'm confident that it was at least twenty feet across.

IMAGE 2
1:14am

The object was still in the same position, but was lit better in this image and it was clear to me that the object had a metallic surface. But the most mysterious aspect of this image was the figure standing next to the object.

At first glance, one may think it to be a thin child in the range of four feet tall. But upon closer inspection, that possibility would be eliminated.

Even though the figure was standing at the far end of the field, the image clearly displays its abnormally large head and black, oval shaped eyes as it stared in the direction of the trail camera.

IMAGE 3
1:27am

The large, metallic object and the humanoid figure are now gone. An average sized deer stands in the center of the field.

IMAGE 4
1:29am

The deer's eyes are opened wide in shock. It is surrounded by a blinding white light coming from somewhere above it out of the camera's range.

The most shocking element of the image is the fact that the deer is suspended in midair.

I couldn't believe what I was seeing.

I hopped on my all-terrain vehicle, motored out to the clearing and inspected it closer.

Everything looked normal. There was nothing out of the ordinary. That is, until I reached the edge of the clearing where the metallic object had been sitting. I found a twenty foot circle burned into the ground.

For the following month after that day, the trail camera did not pick up any images. It was as though the wildlife wanted nothing to do with that area.

Gradually, the animals returned and now things seem to be back to normal in that clearing. But to this day, whenever I ride out to that area, I always find myself gazing up into the sky in fear.

WATCH ME
Rebecca

It had been a rough few weeks for me and I desperately needed a day all to myself. I was overdue for some fun. For me fun equals shopping and eating, so that's what I had planned.

There's an old mall by my house with several clothing stores that I like. I don't frequent them often because most are a little expensive for my taste, but I was treating myself, so I splurged.

My first stop was a store called Abducted by the 80's. I always loved 80's fashion and never understood why it went out of style. To me the store was something of a museum. There were endless racks of bright colored garments, tapered and pleated pants, miniskirts and one piece jumpsuits. There were bracelets, lace gloves, oodles of hair bows and studded belts.

I wound up buying an "off the shoulder" sweatshirt, a bulky sweater and a head band.

While I was waiting with my items at the checkout counter, I noticed a ripped piece of paper with a crudely drawn smiley face on it. When the cashier arrived she asked if the paper was mine. I shook my head and she tossed it away.

From there I headed to the food court. I had a hankering for some French fries so I stopped at a place called Nothing but Fries! They had just about every variety of French fries you could imagine! Waffle fries, curly fries, Belgian fries, steak fries, garlic fries, standard cut, crinkle cut, potato wedges, shoestrings and a lot more! I decided on a big batch of chili cheese fries!

As I sat in the food court munching on my fries and sucking down a cold, soda pop, I could have sworn I heard somebody whisper my name.

"Rebecca."

I looked around but didn't see anybody looking my way, so I didn't think much of it and headed to the next store on my list called The Walk A Mile Shoe Store.

I spent some time browsing and as I found something I liked, I set it on a bench near the front of the store. I picked out some sneakers, boat shoes, flats and knee high boots.

When I sat down and started trying on the various shoes, I noticed a slip of paper stuffed inside one of the boat shoes. I pulled it out and felt my body break out in a chill. The note said: I SEE YOU.

It was topped off with a crude drawing of a smiley face, just like the one I saw at the 80's store.

Was this just some sick joke or was somebody following me?

I looked around the store, but didn't notice anybody suspicious. I walked to the entrance of the store and peered out at the mall for a moment, but nobody was displaying any unusual behavior.

I convinced myself it was nothing to worry about. I certainly wasn't going to let it ruin my day and after purchasing the shoes I wanted, I headed to my favorite store in the mall. I Scream for Ice Cream!

With over fifty unusual flavors to choose from, the novelty ice cream shop sure didn't make my decision easy. Ultimately, I decided on one scoop of rum raisin and one scoop of cinnamon-basil served in a bowl.

I sat down at my favorite booth in the corner of the shop. My ex-boyfriend, Danny, had introduced me to this ice cream shop. This was our favorite booth.

I had promised myself I wouldn't think about him during my alone day, but I knew that was a promise likely to be broken. After all, it was our recent breakup that had made the past few weeks so tough.

Danny and I had been dating for a year. Everything had been going great. He was kind, considerate and rather charming. At least, I thought he was. When we decided to move in together, everything changed. Or maybe nothing changed at all. Perhaps, by living with Danny and seeing him every single day, I was finally seeing him for who he truly was.

I discovered Danny had a short temper. And he never just got angry like normal people did, he exploded. He was like volcano constantly on the verge of erupting. And everything was always somebody else's fault, never his. He could spill a glass of water and find a way to blame it on me.

I learned that Danny wasn't a very sympathetic figure either. If I had a bad day at work and vented to Danny about it, he'd simply nod and then ask what was for dinner or something like that. Everything was always about him. And in all of our time together, Danny never apologized to me. I never heard him say the words, I'm sorry.

Toward the end, I noticed that Danny was usually emotionless and cold. He didn't seem to care about anything. Including me. I knew breaking up with him would be ugly. He'd throw a fit, but it was to the point where I felt like I had to walk on eggshells around him and that's no way to live a life, so I built up the courage and ended it.

It took me a moment, but I finally pushed the thoughts of Danny from my mind and focused on my flavorful ice cream. When I got up and left, I noticed a torn piece of paper lying on the floor just outside the ice cream shop. I didn't have to pick it up to read it. The writing was bold and clear.

Hi Rebecca.

It had to be Danny. He was trying to screw with my head. He was really good at that. But I wasn't going to let him get the best of me. I ignored the note and did a little more mall shopping before I headed home.

When I arrived home, I checked my mail. The only thing in my mailbox was a DVD with a sticky note stuck on the front of it that read, "WATCH ME."

This had to be another one of Danny's stupid stunts. I had the urge to simply throw the DVD away, but my curiosity wouldn't allow it. I reluctantly placed the disc into the player and stood defiantly with my arms crossed as I watched it.

The DVD took a moment to start. It was just a black screen with muffled sound for several seconds before suddenly a shaky image appeared accompanied by the turbulent sound of wind attacking the recording device's microphone.

This was a homemade video. That's why the image was so shaky. I instantly recognized that the video was taken outside the mall and when the camera zoomed in, I recognized myself entering the mall.

The video was from today.

The next shot was taken from inside the mall. It was a shot of me walking into the Abducted by the 80's store. The video then cut to the interior of the store. The camera angle was from behind a row of clothing. Occasionally, a black gloved hand would move some garments over and it would focus on me browsing.

The next shot was a close-up of the checkout counter as the gloved hand placed down the first smiley face picture I encountered.

The next video cut to a zoomed in shot of me wolfing down my chili fries. The loud, distorted audio of the videographer whispering my name reverberated through the room. The shaky camera zoomed in on my French fry filled face as I gazed around bewilderedly.

In the shoe store the video showed the gloved hand place the note that said, I see you, inside the boat shoe. Then it showed the hand place the note with my name on it outside, I Scream For Ice Cream.

The final shot of the video on the DVD was a still photo of a note which read: I'M IN YOUR BEDROOM CLOSET!

At that moment, I heard a loud bang coming from my bedroom. That was meant to frighten me. But it wasn't working. Danny was behind all of this and I was fuming!

I marched into my bedroom. I wasn't going to play his childish games. If anyone was going to be scared it would be him when he found out how furious I was!

As I stomped up to the closet door and reached for the doorknob, the loud ding coming from my cellphone stopped me in my tracks. It was my video doorbell alerting me that someone was outside. This was followed by a knock at the front door. I removed my phone from my pocket and pulled up the live video.

I was shocked when I saw Danny standing outside the front door. But if Danny was outside, who was in my closet?

As that thought entered my mind, the closet door was thrown open and a man donning a black ski mask burst from the closet and attacked me. He shoved me down on my bed and began reaching under my shirt.

I started screaming out for Danny. I knew he heard me as I could hear him yelling out my name as he pounded on the front door. Just as the maniacal man slid his hand under my bra, I heard the loud crack of the front door breaking open, followed by the thudding steps of Danny rushing to my rescue.

Danny grabbed the man and threw him off of me. The two men scuffled, but Danny had the advantage and landed several solid body blows to the masked maniac. Knowing he was in trouble, the attacker pushed Danny away long enough to turn and flee.

I got up from the bed, crying hysterically. I collapsed into Danny's arms. He held me tight and assured me that everything would be all right.

God only knows what would have happened if Danny hadn't showed up.

WATCH ME
Danny

I was shocked when Rebecca broke up with me. I'm good looking, I have a solid job and I'm a pretty nice guy most of the time. I mean, what else does she want?

Rebecca called me crazy during our final argument. She sounded like that bitch psychiatrist I was forced to see when I was 13 years old after I accidentally cut a girl with a knife.

The psychiatrist claimed that I had sociopathic tendencies. But what did she know? Some fancy schmancy degree gives her the right to call me crazy? She was full of shit! If you ask me, she was the one with the problem. She probably called all of her patients crazy to make her feel better about herself because she was the one who was really insane! Stupid bitch!

I never forgot what that psychiatrist said. I waited patiently for a few years until I was no longer associated with her and nobody would tie her death to me. And then I took care of her.

I thought about taking care of Rebecca too. She was mine and if I couldn't have her, nobody could! She was either going to take me back or I'd end her. Of course, I knew getting her back wouldn't be easy, so I had to devise something cunning. I had to do something for her to view me as a knight in shining armor as opposed to some whacko.

I followed her and recorded her throughout her "alone" day. I also dropped little notes to make her suspect that someone was stalking her. I knew there was a better than average chance that Rebecca would think it was me that was doing the stalking, so I needed an accomplice. I got my good friend James to do me the favor of playing the attacker.

James is a great guy. He wanted to help me, but was reluctant to get so physical with Rebecca. It took a lot of persuading, but eventually I was able to convince James that what he was doing would be great for me and Rebecca in the long run.

My plan worked like a charm. Rebecca took me back.

My focus then shifted to James. He was the only one who knew that I was behind it all. He could blackmail me if he wanted. Of course, he never would. James was a great guy. He'd keep his mouth shut, I had no doubt about that. But I couldn't take any chances, so I took care of James. I had to. I had to do it for the sake of my future with Rebecca.

My relationship with Rebecca would be different this time. I knew what I had to do to keep her. I'd keep my temper hidden and I'd never let her see me angry. I fancied myself a decent actor so I'd have no problem pretending to care when she complained about the petty issues from her work days. If she was upset with me I'd tell her I was sorry, even if I wasn't. I'd act like I was happy, cheerful and thoughtful even if my feelings were dead inside.

I was confident that Rebecca and I would live happily ever after.

I FOUND AN ELEVATOR IN THE MIDDLE OF A FOREST

I'm a hiking enthusiast. It's what I do for relaxation. I live close to a trail town and every evening after dinner, I spend at least an hour hiking one of the nearby trails.

At least once a year, I take a nice long vacation to a remote location all by my lonesome. And what do I do on those vacations? You guessed it. I go hiking.

Everyone's definition of "remote" is different. For some city folks, remote simply means the wilderness, regardless of how many people are trampling about. For others it means, seeing the occasional fellow vacationer, just not too many of them. And then there are people like me whose idea of remote equals no sign of humanity for as far as the eye can see.

I'm not a survivalist or a camper. I like to stay in a lodge or a cabin with plenty of food and drinks and hike the surrounding area.

Truly remote locations can be costly, but I think they're worth every penny. Over the years, I've done several of these types of hikes. I've been in areas one can only get to via helicopter. One trip I took required a one hour mule ride to get to the cabin.

The cabin I rented for my latest excursion was only accessible by boat. It was small, but cozy. It was powered by a propane generator. It didn't have much in the way of amenities, but it had all I needed. A stocked refrigerator, running water, a stovetop and a fireplace for chilly nights.

The cabin was amidst the most beautiful snowcapped mountains I had ever seen. The air was cool, crisp and clean. There was no humidity. It was the kind of weather that would allow me to hike deep into the surrounding wilderness without getting winded.

I had rented the cabin for a full week. The first two days, I hiked near the cabin. The third day I ventured farther. The fourth day, I went deep into the darkest depths of the surrounding forest. The thickness of the treetops cast a gloomy shadow over everything. Even though it was mid-afternoon, the section of forest I found myself in held the image and mood of dusk.

As I stopped to rest and gaze about at the unusually dim-lit surroundings, I leaned up against a western red cedar tree, one of the thickest trees in the country.

As I leaned against it, the tree trunk seemed to give slightly.

That was strange. It felt as though the tree were artificial in the spot I put my weight against. I studied the front of the tree closely and could barely make out the thin perimeter of what appeared to be a door. It was camouflaged to near perfection. Had I not leaned against it, I would have walked right past it without giving it a second glance.

Why was there a door hidden within a tree?

I started feeling my way around the tree. Most of it felt like a real tree should, solid, sturdy and heavy. It was only the door section that felt synthetic. But I did notice a branch next to the door that seemed out of place. The bark was slightly smoother and darker than the rest of the tree. When I reached up and grasped the branch, it gave way and lowered slightly before springing back into place. This was immediately followed by the bark camouflaged doors sliding open to reveal a solid, metallic door.

An elevator door.

I instinctively looked around the forest to see if I noticed anyone watching me, but there was nobody. I was alone in the forest staring at an elevator that was hidden within a tree.

What the hell was this?

I noticed a plastic green button next to the door. I had to press it, right? I couldn't just walk away and pretend I never saw this. It was too strange. I had to investigate.

I could feel goosebumps tingle my arms as I reached out and pressed the green button. Within a few seconds I heard a mechanical rumble and watched the elevator doors slide open. The interior of the elevator was metallic chrome just as the elevator door was.

I stared at the open elevator for a moment and studied it. It was shiny and spotless clean. I poked my head inside and looked around. I could see a small panel on one side of the elevator doors. It had only one, non-labeled button on it.

I was more than slightly apprehensive about getting inside. I spoke my initial hesitation aloud.

"What if the elevator gets stuck?"

But I was the adventurous type. I wasn't going to pass up the opportunity to find out where the elevator led to, so I slowly, cautiously stepped into the elevator.

Nothing happened. I stood in the elevator facing the doors which remained open. I took in a deep breath as I reached out and pressed the button.

Still nothing.

That's when I noticed a small key dangling from a keyhole underneath elevator's lone button. I carefully turned the key and it stopped with a click. I then pressed the button again and suddenly the elevator rumbled to life and silence was shattered by the whoosh of elevator cables sliding the elevator deep down into the ground. Several seconds later, the elevator stopped and the doors slid open.

The first thing I noticed was a small lamp with a red shade sitting atop a whiskey barrel. It was sitting against a dark green wall approximately five feet in front of me. To the left I could see a solid brick wall. I poked my head out of the elevator and looked to my right. There was a long hallway.

I had come this far, there was no turning back now, so I exited the elevator.

I slowly began walking down the hallway. It was approximately fifty feet long. It was smooth and painted dark green. Every ten feet or so was a modern wall lamp that highlighted the various rusty advertising signs that were decorating the hallway walls.

This was somebody's home. But who and why?

The hallway emptied into a spacious living room. There was a nice beige, u-shaped sectional couch adorning the center of the room. There were various throw pillows placed on it. A square coffee table was positioned in front of the couch. It was all centered around a large screen TV.

I noticed an antique stand up radio at one corner of the room. A framed picture sat on top of the radio. It showed a man, who I assumed to be the owner of the home, in hunter's gear, holding a rifle while standing over the dead body of a hulking moose.

The picture made perfect sense when I scanned the décor of the living room. The walls were lined with the mounted trophy heads of the various animals this man had evidently killed over the years. Deer, elk, bear, wild hog, buffalo, cougar, bobcat…I gasped and momentarily choked on my own saliva when I saw it.

It was a human head mounted up there with the rest of the animal kingdom.

"Holy shit."

I peered back over at the picture of the man standing over the moose. He was a big bulky man. I wouldn't fair well against him in hand to hand combat. It was probably just dumb luck that I happened across his hidden home when he wasn't around. I needed to get out of there and fast!

I bolted down the hallway, rushed into the elevator and prayed that it would take me back up. I pressed the button and fortunately the elevator started its ascent.

The ride up seemed a lot longer than the ride down, but finally the elevator came to a stop and the doors rattled opened. I feared the human killing hunter would be standing there and I expelled an audible breath of relief when all I saw was forest in front of me.

I hurried out of the elevator and pulled the fake limb down. The elevator door closed tight followed by the false tree door.

I made it to safety. Or so I thought.

I swear every organ in my body momentarily shut down when I heard heavy footsteps plodding through the crispy dead leaves lining the forest floor.

I had to be careful. If I ran, he'd hear me. He likely had a high powered rifle on him and could shoot me down with no problem!

I took slow, soft steps away from the elevator tree and inched my way toward the shield of another huge tree nearby. The footsteps were getting louder. Closer. He was almost on me.

Every fiber of my body urged me to pick up the pace, but I remained true to my strategy and moved ever so carefully so as not to make a sound. I ducked behind a tree just as the brawny man came into view.

I took in slow shallow breaths, but my heart was beating so fast and hard, I wouldn't have been shocked if he heard it!

I wanted to peek to confirm that the man was not aware of my presence, but I didn't dare. I just plastered myself behind the shield of the tree and listened.

I could hear the squeak of the branch device as he pulled it followed by the mechanical whoosh of the elevator doors opening. It was only when the elevator doors closed and I could hear gears grinding as it sent the elevator down to the man's secret home, that I felt brave enough to look.

If the man knew I was there, he'd likely send the elevator down to make me feel at ease enough to show my face and he'd be standing there waiting for me. But luckily, that was not the case. He wasn't there. The coast was clear.

I dashed through the forest back to my cabin and immediately called the folks who ran the getaway retreat. I told them that I was extremely ill, so I had to cut my vacation short and for them to send a boat to come get me.

I didn't dare tell them what I found. For all I knew the people who ran the getaway retreat knew the killer and the head on his wall was that of the last guy who stumbled across his lair and blabbed about it.

No sir.

I kept my trap shut and I never said a word to anyone.

THE THING AT THE BOTTOM OF THE LAKE

I used to dive for fun. Now I do it for a living.

I dive to the bottom of rivers, lakes and oceans and look for valuable items that I can turn around and sell. Over the years I've found expensive jewelry, gold, arrowheads, cannon balls, cash, megalodon teeth, shipwrecks, diamonds and other rare gems, dinosaur fossils and much more.

I've also discovered some rather unusual items such as a prosthetic leg, countless guns, a car, a very creepy porcelain doll, a tombstone that was over one hundred years old, multiple human skulls and one full human skeleton.

My latest diving adventure took me to a massive lake in Tennessee known as Shadow Lake which was known for the excessive amount of people who had gone missing while visiting the lake. The amount of missing person cases of people visiting the Shadow Lake area had increased substantially over the past thirty years. Nobody knows for sure as to why.

It is theorized that the incredible depths of Shadow Lake, which houses countless underwater caverns, was the likely culprit for the majority of the disappearances. It was easy to get lost if exploring the caverns and drown. That theory seemed extremely plausible.

As callous as it may sound, lots of missing people equaled lots of potential valuable items to find. And who knows, I may happen upon a body or two and that could help to solve some of those missing person cases.

The first thing that I noticed when I sank deep into the depths of Shadow Lake was how incredibly dark it was. Even with my extreme bright underwater light, visibility was near zero. But I trekked on and did find some worthwhile items.

I found a gold wedding ring with a nice sized diamond. If the diamond was real, this would fetch a decent amount of money. I also found a thick, gold necklace. It wasn't worth near as much as the ring, but it was still valuable.

Financially, those finds were nice, but I found something else that was much more interesting.

A piece of wood.

Water is not wood's friend, but somehow this broken piece of wood found a way to remain near perfectly preserved.

The wood itself was nothing exciting. It was about three feet by three feet. The edges were jagged indicating this was just a piece of a larger object. Likely a box of some kind.

The fascinating thing about the wood was the stenciling on the front of it that read: ARCTIC EXPEDITION

There was a date under the words. I couldn't read the month or day, they were too smudged. But the year clearly read as 1834.

Now, obviously that thing hadn't been in the lake since 1834. No way. But still, it was incredibly intriguing.

I began scanning the lake floor around that area for any other remnants of the box in hopes to garner further information about it, but I couldn't find anything. I did however, find an enormous underwater cave. I have seen some impressive caverns under the water before, but this cave opening was gigantic. It had to be twenty feet tall.

I swam into the cave and found that it kept its impressive size as I traveled down it. I was probably two hundred feet into it when I noticed that there were multiple, thinner passages that snaked off from the main cave. I swam into the closest one.

Even though the cavern passage was much smaller than the cave it was housed within, it was still well over six feet tall and eight feet across, I had no problem swimming through it and I was shocked at how deep it went. It seemed as though it were never ending!

Just ahead, I noticed another passageway and quickly realized how easy it would be for someone to get lost within the labyrinth of tunnels. My plan was to take a quick gaze into the adjoining passage and then head back before I got too far, but what I saw inside the opening of the passage made me panic.

It was a gigantic pile of human bones. Most of them were shattered and crushed in places. It was clear that something had ravaged them.

But what?

I wasn't going to wait around to find out and I swam as fast as I could out of the passage, through the main cave and back into the depths of Shadow Lake.

I tried to keep calm, but wasn't successful. I was having a full blown anxiety attack as I tried to swim toward the surface of the lake. Bubbles of oxygen were clouding my face and I could hear my own screams of terror when I felt something latch around my ankle.

I shined my light down and saw a massive hand with long, thick claws wrapped around my lower leg. When I moved the light over to see the beast that was attached to the claw, I instantly regretted it.

The creature was covered in dirty, white fur. When I first caught a glimpse of its face I thought it had the appearance of a gorilla until it opened its huge mouth and revealed rows of sabre-like teeth.

Somehow I managed to kick out of its grip and I shot like a missile through the water until I broke the surface. I was screaming the entire time I swam toward shore knowing that any second I was likely to be dragged down into the depths of Shadow Lake by that hideous monster.

What was that thing? Could that ancient piece of wood I found be a clue as to where it came from? I'd likely never know the answers to those questions. Especially if I didn't survive the day!

I was nothing short of shocked when I made it to the shore, but it didn't slow me down. I ran as far away from Shadow Lake as I could before collapsing from exhaustion.

I called the police and told them of my discovery of the bones and the creature that attacked me. They sent down a team of divers but couldn't find the cave I spoke of. I somehow summoned the courage to dive down with them, and I led them to the cave, but refused to follow them inside.

They found the pile of bones. After extensive testing they concluded that most of the bones belonged to the people who had gone missing from the area.

The divers never found any sign of the creature I encountered. But it's down there somewhere, hiding within the endless caverns of Shadow Lake that it calls home.

A DREAM COME TRUE

I dream about her every night.

We're walking through a grassy green meadow which is sprinkled with hints of yellow. There is a gentle breeze that flows through her golden hair. Her cherry red lips part revealing a cheerful smile. It takes me a moment to work up the courage to reach out and take her hand into mine, but I do it and she's receptive. Our future together is bright.

And then I wake up.

For the first few seconds of being awake, I'm still filled with the thrill of love I feel within the dream, but I quickly descend into a dark place when I realize none of it was real.

She's not real.

I find myself in a depressed mood for the majority of days and they drag on forever. Nights are better because I know I'll be drifting off into the dream world soon and I'll see her again. And perhaps the dream will move farther along and I'll see what comes next.

But it never does.

The dream is always us in a meadow and I wake up shortly after we are hand in hand.

For the longest time I was content with the perfect moment of us joining hands and walking through the meadow, but as time went on, I found myself wanting more.

The dreams that were the only thing in my mundane life that I looked forward to were not enough. I needed more. I needed to know what happened next.

My depression grew more intense. I felt like I was sinking into a bottomless pit. I began contemplating the way I would end it all.

And then I saw her.

I was walking past a park on my way to work when I saw her sitting alone at a picnic table. Her golden hair draped her shoulders. Her head was drooped down and I detected her sadness.

But it was her. It was without question the girl of my dreams.

I don’t know how long I stood there gawking at her, but eventually she sensed it and looked up at me and I saw the recognition in her eyes. This was followed by her cherry lips parting and that sunbeam of a smile shining through.

She ran to me and came to an abrupt halt when she was within arm’s reach.

“Is it you?”

She knew me.

“It’s me. Is it you? Is it really you? Are you the girl of my dreams?”

Her eyes welled up with tears and she hugged me tightly. Time stopped as we embraced. It was like two long lost lovers reuniting after years apart.

After our embrace reached its conclusion, I stared into her crystal blue eyes.

“I can’t believe it’s you. It’s really you! You’re real.”

She stared back at me. She held her mesmerizing smile as she studied every contour of my face, even reaching out and touching it ever so gently on occasion. Finally she spoke.

“Let’s live the dream.”

I knew what she meant. It was time to walk hand and hand in the meadow and see where the dream led to.

We found ourselves walking down a dirt path as if being guided by the dream itself. I can't say I was surprised when we stepped through a line of trees and found ourselves in the meadow. The very meadow I dreamed of night after night.

I felt like we were moving in slow motion as we walked through the grassy green meadow, sprinkled with hints of yellow. The gentle breeze flowing softly through her golden hair. Her cherry red lips parted and revealed that cheerful smile. My heart began to flutter as I worked up the courage to reach out and take her hand into mine, but I did it. Just like I always did in the dream. And she accepted it.

I came to an abrupt halt and it confused her.

"What's wrong?"

"This is where my dream always ends. I don't know what happens next."

She let out a playful laugh.

"I do."

Her smile and confidence reassured me and I allowed her to lead me though the meadow and into a forest.

The forest was dark and dreary and she stopped when we came upon an old cemetery that was littered with unmarked graves.

"This is where the dream ends."

I was staring into her stunning eyes when she put her hand into her purse, withdrew a hammer and slammed it into the top of my head. I fell to the ground in a daze, but I was able to hear her lovely voice as she bent down and gazed at me.

"Your dream was a nightmare and you didn't even realize it."

Her gorgeous face never became enraged or psychotic in any way. She continued to hold that striking smile as she carved me to pieces. She stared as me lovingly as she spoke.

"But for me, you're a dream come true."

CANCER
The Patient

"I need a miracle."

I had been diagnosed with stage 4, inoperable stomach cancer. I got second opinions, third opinions, fourth opinions, but they all agreed. I had no more than three months to live.

I didn't feel like it was my time. I was only 33 years old. I had so many things I still wanted to do.

If there was a bright side, it was that I didn't have a wife or kids and my loving parents died when I was in my early 20's so there was nobody close to me that my passing would devastate.

I begged the doctors to give me some hope. I insisted that there must be some kind of treatment that might cure me. Some of the doctors said we could try aggressive chemo and radiation therapy. Others said that would be akin to torturing myself and encouraged me to simply enjoy the remainder of my life while I could.

I didn't want to waste time with treatments that would bring me nothing but misery, but I also wasn't willing to go down without a fight. I was desperate and began looking into every conceivable option possible.

I found myself in the office of a holistic doctor. He told me the best he could do was give me something for the pain. I told him I was only interested in being cured.

The doctor paused for a long while as if contemplating something. At this stage of my life every second counted.

"What? What is it?"

The holistic doctor continued to hesitate but finally came forth with his thoughts.

"I know someone. He's not a doctor. He's a scientist. His grandmother died from cancer. His mother died from cancer. His wife died from cancer. Now, cancer is his obsession. He dedicates every waking second of his life to finding a cure. His problem is that he needs people to experiment on."

For the first time since I had been diagnosed with cancer, I felt a surge of hope rush through my veins.

"You're saying he needs a human guinea pig."

The holistic doctor shrugged.

"Yes. I suppose that's what I'm saying."

"I'm in!"

The location I was given was an old, abandoned clinic. The sidewalk was overrun by weeds. The mundane exterior of the three story building was weathered and cracked.

After rapping my knuckles on the mildew stained glass door, it was the scientist himself who answered. He was a short, balding man wearing an unbuttoned dress shirt, a sloppy neck tie and a stained lab coat. His gray eyebrows were bushy and the creases in his forehead were prominent. His resting face held that of a subtle scowl.

When I told him I needed a miracle, the man affixed his cold, icy blue eyes on me. He showed no signs of emotion as he spoke.

"Every second you're alive is a miracle. My goal is to provide you with more of those precious seconds. But let me be perfectly clear, I want to experiment on you. I can guarantee you nothing in the way of results."

"Can you guarantee me that you'll try your best to cure me?"

I thought I sensed a subtle smirk from the scientist.

"Yes, I can guarantee you that."

"Then we have a deal."

I spent a couple hours signing all kinds of forms that made it clear that I was agreeing to these experiments willingly. It would likely keep the scientist out of jail if these secret experiments ever got out to the public.

The scientist wasted no time. He set me up in a small hospital room which was much cleaner than the rest of the building's innards. I was set up to an IV immediately and he rattled off the list of ingredients that were mixed in the bag that was dripping into my veins. Some of it sounded like medicine and some sounded like fruit. The only thing that sounded familiar to me was avocado extract.

The scientist explained that the mixture would likely cause side effects. Due to the lack of human subjects he wasn't positive what I would experience but said the common side effects would be varying degrees of anxiety, nervousness, fear and panic.

Twelve hours later, those side effects were in full swing. I wasn't sure what I was so nervous and anxious about but the fact that the scientist was coming into the room nearly every hour was certainly contributing to it.

He kept fidgeting with the IV bag and would periodically add a syringe full of liquid to it. He didn't speak much. Would it kill him to ask me how I felt once in a while?

Every few hours he would take blood from my veins. Why did he need so much? What was he doing? I was sure that I'd feel better about the procedure if he would keep me updated, but the man was practically mute. There was also something scary about him. I couldn't quite place my finger on it yet, but there was something worth fearing with him. That much I knew.

The following day, I was surprised when the scientist opened his mouth and graced me with his voice.

"How much pain were you in when you arrived yesterday?"

"Constant pain. Nothing I can't handle. It feels like a mild cramp in my stomach."

"And what about now? How much pain are you in now?"

I was shocked. I hadn't even realized that the pain in my stomach had vanished.

"It's…it's gone. It's gone! What does this mean?"

"Nothing yet. But it's a step in the right direction. With your permission, I'd like to up the dosage of this medicine to a much higher level. A level I have never administered to anyone before."

"Do whatever you need to."

It was less than an hour when the scientist upped the dose to a much more potent level.

The effects were strange. I felt numb and tingly before I passed out. I dreamt of the scientist hovering over me with surgical instruments in his hands. I could feel the pressure of him slicing through my flesh and removing my internal organs.

I woke up in a cold sweat. My stomach was aching. I reached down and could feel a long line of stitches running along my stomach and my lower back.

It wasn't a dream I was having. It was a memory.

He was taking my organs!

This son of a bitch wasn't a scientist! It was all a ruse to sedate me and steal my organs so he could sell them on the black market!

I ripped the IV out of my arm, leapt from my bed and exited my room. I raced up and down the hallway searching for the mad scientist who did this to me. He would pay for this! He would pay dearly!

I saw a room at the end of the hall with light emitting from underneath the door. I hurried to the door and kicked it open.

There he was. The mad scientist. He was sitting at a messy desk amongst towers of cluttered papers. There was a computer monitor in front of him illuminating his evil face.

He scowled at me and I swear his expression didn't change one single bit when I shouted at him.

"You took out my internal organs!"

As I rushed toward him, he turned and reached out for something near his keyboard. A gun no doubt. He had my organs and there was no reason for him to keep me alive any longer! He was going to shoot me dead, so I had no choice but to defend myself.

I strangled him to death with his own neck tie and then I burned his entire clinic to the ground!

CANCER
The Scientist

Cancer is a monster. I am the slayer.

Since my wife's demise, I have dedicated my entire life to finding a way to rid the monstrosity from the face of the earth.

I felt like I was as close as I could get without working with human subjects.

Experimenting on them.

I put word out with every doctor that I trusted to let any terminally ill cancer patients know about me. With each patient I could experiment on, the closer I could get to conquering the beast.

The experimental patients were few and far between but I made great strides with each one.

When the 33 year old man with stomach cancer arrived at my clinic, I was confident he could be the breakthrough patient.

And I was correct.

The first administration of the medicine I concocted had staggering results. According to the blood results his cancer had diminished significantly. The patient agreed to allow me to increase the dosage to levels I had never used before.

From there it was a matter of waiting and observing.

My magic potion, as I like to call it, consists of a perfect balance of various medicines, both pharmaceutical and herbal holistic, along with extracts from numerous fruits and vegetables. Some of the extract is used in psychedelics and can have extreme side effects.

The patient passed out quickly once the heavy dose was administered. This was good because I wasn't sure how extreme the side effects would be. The psychedelic effects coupled with common anxiety and fear side effects could result in dangerous behavior.

After I finished checking his latest blood results, I decided I would put restraints on the patient, just to be on the safe side.

That plan along with everything else in my mind was pushed aside when I saw the results.

The blood test showed no indication of cancer in the patient. None.

I had done it. I had found the cure for cancer!

I'm what the kids may refer to as "old school." I write all my notes down by hand. I was trembling with excitement as I transferred the hand written notes to a computer document that I could save.

I had just typed the last line of the document and was about to press the save button on the keyboard that would automatically send the formula of the magic potion to several colleagues along with it automatically uploading to a secure cloud server to ensure its existence, when the door to my office burst open and the patient lashed out at me.

"You took out my internal organs!"

The patient was hallucinating badly and had become violent. This side effect likely wouldn't last longer than four hours, but that did me no good in the current situation!

As the mad patient rushed me, I turned and reached out to press the send button on the keyboard, but the patient reached me before I could do so.

We struggled for a moment before he wrapped my own tie around my neck and began squeezing the life from me.

It was clear to me that I was going to expire before I could save the cancer curing formula. But I died feeling content knowing that one of my colleagues would find the formula on my computer and the cure for cancer would be obtained.

That is as long as the patient didn't do anything crazy like burn the entire clinic to the ground.

I CAN READ YOUR MIND

My name is Scottie. I'm a senior in high school and I'm a bit of an outcast. Nobody would mistake me for a male model. I have a lot of pimples and crooked front teeth. My hair is short and dyed blue and I'm somewhat overweight although I do plan on losing it soon.

Most people who know me would describe me as the little boy who would never grow up. For example, lots of boys love to climb trees. At some point most of them grow out of that phase of their life. But I never did.

I lived a block away from my high school and walked to and fro every day. Clyde was an acquaintance of mine who lived down the street from me. We weren't friends. We just sometimes walked home together and would occasionally chit chat.

It was Clyde who dared me to climb the massive Siberian Elm tree we passed by every day. He honestly didn't think I could do it. I proved him wrong. I climbed up that thing like a monkey. On my way down, my grip slipped and I fell to the ground with the loudest of thuds and everything went dark.

My ears were ringing with thousands of voices. Gradually the voices departed until I could just hear one. It was Clyde.

Oh no! If he's dead I'll be in so much trouble! I was the one who dared him!

I opened my eyes and stared at Clyde with disdain.

"You thought I might be dead and all you care about is that you might be in trouble?"

Clyde seemed confused.

"What? What are you talking about?"

"I just heard you. I heard what you said."

He shook his head.

"I didn't say anything."

As I got up and started brushing myself off, I noticed that Clyde was looking at me weirdly.

"What? What is it?"

How did he know what I was thinking?

I was staring at Clyde as I heard those words, but his mouth never moved. When it finally did, he was backing away from me.

"I'm going to walk home a different way today."

I watched on as Clyde hurried away from me.

That was strange.

As I continued walking down the sidewalk toward home, a woman in her 30's was coming from the other direction. As she got closer to me she glanced my way.

Boy, he sure is ugly.

I stopped in my tracks. I heard her voice, but her lips didn't move. When she noticed me staring at her she gave me a polite smile.

"Hi. How are you?"

I just nodded back and she walked past me. She was so polite when she spoke to me. But she had just called me ugly…without moving her lips.

What the hell?

Nice blue hair. Weirdo.

That statement was directed at me from a middle-aged man sitting in a chair outside a store. He was staring at me and his expression concurred with the statement, only he never moved his lips.

I stopped and looked at him.

What's this weirdo gawking at me for?

Again, it was him. It was the man in the chair. I heard him loud and clear…but he wasn't talking! I couldn't help but continue to stare at him in disbelief. He gave me a dirty look as he got up and entered the store.

Damn, I don't have enough change for the parking meter.

This statement came from the woman by the side of the road who was fishing through her purse.

Now I'll have to find another parking spot and I'll be late for my meeting!

I clearly heard her saying these things, but she wasn't talking.

I walked up to the woman and held a baffled expression as I looked at her. She looked up at me and seemed confused.

Who is this?

Again, I could hear her, but she wasn't speaking.

I reached into my pants pocket, pulled out some change and put it into the meter for her. A huge smile took over her face.

"Thank you so much!"

I nodded.

"Sure."

What a nice boy.

That's what I heard as she smiled at me. She didn't say it. I suppose she just…thought it.

That's when it dawned on me. I was reading people's minds! I could hear their thoughts!

I didn't go straight home that day. I meandered around town to test my theory and it was proven correct, quickly. I could hear everything everybody was thinking!

It must have had something to do with my head hitting the ground when I fell out of that tree.

Over the next week I just sat around and blankly listened to people's thoughts. It was my way of accepting that it was all real. This was a legitimate ability that I now possessed.

I took some time to ponder what to do with my newfound ability. Ultimately, I opted for patience. I'd take things slow and figure it out as I'd go.

It was when I was sitting in my least favorite class, history, that I heard something cryptic.

I'm going to kill him.

I looked around the class until I spotted him.

Dexter.

He was a quiet, loner who sat at the back of the class. He didn't have any friends. He sat alone at lunch. Nobody ever talked to him.

I'm going to steal my father's gun and kill Mr. Barlow. I'm really going to do it.

Mr. Barlow was our history teacher. He was a first-class asshole. He was on a constant power trip. He took pleasure in belittling his students. Dexter was one of his favorite targets. He referred to him as a loser and a friendless freak.

Mr. Barlow was the reason I hated history class. He was such a jerk. He picked on me too. He'd occasionally call me chubby and pizza face. But since I was a straight A student, he usually directed his vile remarks at kids who were struggling with their grades.

The next few days I made a point to stay in close vicinity to Dexter and listen to his thoughts. It was depressing to say the least. Dexter spent most of his days trying to work up the courage to engage in conversation with other kids in school, but he'd always chicken out. What he wanted more than anything was a friend. I got the impression that if he just had a good friend, he wouldn't become the killer that he was otherwise destined to be. So one day I talked to him.

I was always different and didn't have a lot of friends myself, so it was easy for me to relate to him. I think he appreciated that. It took a little while to get him to come out of his shell, but once he did he was a nice, friendly kid.

My passion in life is collecting toy action figures. The older the better. One day I wanted to open my own collectibles store and auction house. I had the college that would teach me how to achieve my dream all picked out. It was a tough school to get into, but my grades were impeccable so it wouldn't be a problem.

Dexter really took to my toy collection. I could see a similar passion brewing within the young man that I had. I have to admit, I was a bit proud of him.

As Dexter and I became closer friends, Dexter's homicidal thoughts toward Mr. Barlow began to decrease. He no longer thought about actually killing Mr. Barlow. He shifted his thoughts to hoping Mr. Barlow would fall down a flight of stairs or get into a car accident. But he was no longer contemplating murder.

One day after leaving history class, I realized I forgot one of my other school books at my desk. When I stepped into the classroom to retrieve it, I saw Mr. Barlow sitting at his desk grading our final exams.

"What do you want? I'm busy!"

"Sorry Mr. Barlow, I just forgot one of my books on my desk..."

"Get it and get the hell out of here!"

As I walked to my desk, Mr. Barlow went on a tirade in his mind. About me!

Oh, how I would love to flunk that chubby, ugly, pimple faced brainiac. But he aced his history exam. That means he'll get an A in this class and have straight A's all throughout high school. He'll have his pick of colleges. But this little punk doesn't realize that I have all the power. I hold his future in my hands! All I have to do is change a few of his answers on the exam and he'll wind up with a B instead of an A. Let's see how that blue haired geek feels about that!

I couldn't believe what I was hearing! This power crazed teacher was going to manipulate my test scores and ruin my perfect high school record!

The college of my choice would accept me without question if I had straight A's. If there was a B on my record that would drop me a level and it would no longer be a given!

I might be able to live with that if the grade was legitimate, but this was all going to be at the hands of a lunatic teacher!

I had to do something! I couldn't let this psycho ruin my future! Dammit, if I had never befriended Dexter, maybe he would have killed Mr. Barlow and this wouldn't be happening.

That's when I got a bright idea. I walked with determination to Dexter's locker. When he turned around he smiled. That's when I let him have it.

"I hate you Dexter. You're good for nothing. Mr. Barlow was right about you. You're a loser and friendless freak."

I could see sadness welling within his eyes as he spoke.

"But…but you're my friend, Scottie."

"Let me make this loud and clear so there is no misunderstanding. I am not your friend! And I never will be!"

This devastated Dexter and later that day he killed Mr. Barlow.

Being that Mr. Barlow didn't live long enough to finish grading the final exams, the principal took up that task.

I got the A that I deserved and was accepted into the college of my choice.

MY SCARIEST CLIENT

I'm a retired criminal defense attorney. In my day I defended some of the meanest, most intimidating people in society. Thieves, kidnappers, carjackers, sexual deviants, arsonists, rapists, and of course, murders.

The scariest client I ever defended was a murderer, but he wasn't some hulking, heavily tattooed cretin. He was a good looking young man in his late 20's. He was of average size, but was in very good shape. He had wavy blonde hair and pale blue eyes. He was also very intelligent. His name was Ellis Cole.

The scariest thing about Mr. Cole was how detached he was. I never saw him display anger, fear, sadness, joy or any other emotion. He was completely charmless. Not once did I seem him crack the slightest of smiles. When I looked into his eerie eyes I saw nothing. No spark. No conscience. No Soul.

Ellis Cole was a cash register repairman. He worked at several different stores in various locations. He was accused of butchering and killing four women. All four women worked at stores that Ellis Cole worked at. There are witnesses that say he asked two of them out and they declined due to his unsettling aura.

Ellis had decent alibies for all four murders. Not rock solid, but decent. It was enough that the detectives on the case would have to come up with some serious evidence to put him away.

And serious evidence they found.

Blood that matched the blood type of one of his victims was found on his clothing. This was the late 1980's. DNA testing had not yet been established. Blood found on Ellis Cole's clothing that happened to match the same blood type of one of the victims would likely be enough to put him away for life or possibly send him to the electric chair.

I hated being alone with Ellis Cole. He'd stare at me no matter what we were doing. And he wouldn't move. It was like sitting in the room with a damned mannequin. It was unnerving.

When I told him of the evidence that was found he replied immediately.

"They're lying."

His voice was dry, monotone and colorless. It matched his demeanor. With each word he uttered a chill moved further down my spine.

"I want to make sure you understand that I'm not confessing to killing those women. All I'm saying is if I had killed them, I wouldn't have worn clothing while committing the act. I would have been completely naked so as to make sure there was no chance of their blood staining my clothes."

By the time he was finished I was covered in goosebumps.

He killed those girls. I had no doubt in my mind that he was guilty. And yet, it was my job to defend him to the best of my ability. And I did.

Regretfully, I did.

Obviously the detectives on the case were convinced Ellis Cole was guilty but knew they didn't have the evidence to put him away, so they manufactured it.

The detectives wouldn't be dumb enough to obtain the blood to plant on Ellis Cole's clothes from the crime lab. They'd have to sign in. They couldn't leave such obvious tracks, so I got my private investigator on the job.

My P.I. found out that one of the detectives was dating a lab technician in a local hospital. He obtained video surveillance footage of the detective sneaking into the blood lab one day while visiting her. More than that, the video showed him leaving the room holding a small vial of blood.

This was enough to create a shadow of a doubt and Ellis Cole was set free onto the world.

I was relieved when I found out that Ellis Cole immediately moved out of the state. But I was frightened for whatever town that monster settled in.

Who knows how many more victims he claimed over the years?

That's something I have to live with.

BOOK OF HORRORS

Sam's Secure Storage is a massive indoor storage facility. It's by far the biggest in the Western Kentucky and probably the entire state and surrounding region. Hell, I've never seen a bigger one.

Every few months, the owner, who everyone affectionately refers to as Old Sam, holds a storage locker auction. In case you didn't know, if someone rents a storage locker and stops paying, the storage facility will attempt to contact them. If after a suitable amount of time the party in question does not respond or pay, the storage facility will auction off the unit. Whoever wins the auction gains ownership of everything within that unit. Most storage facilities give the auction winners 24 to 72 hours to clear out the storage unit. Sam's Secure Storage allows 24 hours.

A lot of the folks who show up to these auctions buy and sell items for a living. That's not me. I'm a collector. I only buy storage units if I'm confident there may be some serious collectibles dwelling within.

Don't get me wrong, if the collectible is valuable and doesn't speak to me, I'm not against selling it for a hefty profit, but that's not my initiative. My goal is to add to my growing collection of interesting conversation pieces.

The way these auctions work is they will open the door to the storage unit being sold and let you look for a few minutes, but nobody is allowed to go inside. So if a storage unit is filled with cardboard boxes, nobody would know if those boxes were full of gold or were completely empty.

I'm not a gambler. I'm the kind of guy who won't bid on anything unless I see something I know I want or am at least curious about.

There were only three units up for auction on this day and the first two didn't have anything that interested me. When the auctioneer pulled open the garage-like door to the final unit of the day, the seasoned bidders let out a harmonic groan of disappointment.

The contents inside the storage unit resembled that of a dumpster. There were a lot of ripped up cardboard boxes that were tossed inside the unit without any care. I saw a myriad of empty, plastic storage containers strewn about, some cheap furniture, a couple of disgusting mattresses and clothes. Mounds upon mounds of dirty clothes.

Nobody wanted this unit. And I concurred. It was nothing but junk.

Or so I thought.

As I peered deep within the back corner of the unit, I noticed a pile of books. I'm sure I wasn't the only one who saw them, but most used books are completely worthless, so that simply added to the undesirable nature of the unit to my bidding competitors.

However, one of the books caught my eye. It was oddly large in size and appeared to have an old, thick leather cover. I had no doubt it was a vintage book. It was likely not worth much and probably not very interesting, but my curiosity was piqued and if the price was right, I might consider throwing my bidding hat into the ring.

The auctioneer opened up asking for a twenty dollar bid.

Crickets.

He dropped it down to fifteen.

Still nothing.

When he offered it up for ten dollars, I raised my hand. Nobody else bid, so the unit was mine!

Once the auction had concluded and everyone else had cleared out, I stepped into the unit I had won and scanned over the contents. Upon closer inspection, mine and everyone else's assumption that the unit was full of rubbish was confirmed. I had to move piles of the soiled clothing out of the unit to clear a path to the mysterious book that I coveted.

It took some work, but I was finally able to reach the book and it was everything I had hoped it would be and then some.

First of all it was big. I figured it to be approximately 16 inches by 16 inches. Very odd dimensions for a book indeed.

The mahogany leather cover was thick and battered. The edges were worn. There were various small tears covering the front, back and spine. This book hadn't been sitting on a shelf its entire life. It had seen some action, for sure.

There was no intricate carving as is seen in many vintage leather books. This cover was crude and unrefined. There was no author name on the book. Just the title which was written in a language that I suspected was Latin.

MORS EST HIC

I didn't know what that translated to and flipped to the first page of the book, which was a flyleaf. In the book world that refers to an empty page at the beginning of a book. Only this page wasn't empty. Someone had scribbled something across the front of it in red ink. I have to admit that I was a little bit rattled by what it said.

THIS BOOK IS CURSED! IF YOU READ IT YOU WILL DIE!

I'm not the superstitious type, but I didn't feel comfortable turning the page, so I shut the book. I was going to bring it to a book dealer I knew in town to see what she thought.

It took me a few hours to clean the remaining trash out of the storage unit. By the time I was finished it was dark and I was certain I was the only one there. After taking the last of the garbage out to the dumpster, I returned for the book.

Sam's Secure Storage building was creepy when no one else was around. The halls were lined with emotionless, gray metal storage doors. The walls themselves were constructed of cinderblock that was covered in tattered, flaking green paint. To top it all off, half of the fluorescent bulbs lighting the hall were burned out. The one in front of my locker was flickering.

I just wanted to grab the book and get out of there. I was getting a serious case of the heebie-jeebies!

As I approached the unit, I paused to make sure I heard what I thought I had.

Breathing.

It was heavy, rhythmic breathing coming from inside my storage unit. From my vantage point, I wouldn't be able to see within the locker unless I was standing directly in front of it. I was hesitant to do so in fear that someone might be in there waiting to bushwhack me, so I called out.

"Hello?"

There was no response. I listened for a several seconds and didn't hear anything else. Not even the breathing. The only thing I could hear was the chaotic buzz of the flickering light overhead.

"Listen, I have a gun. If you try anything, I'm going to start shooting."

I was lying. I wished I had been carrying a gun, but I wasn't.

I waited a good couple of minutes before I dashed out in front of the storage unit.

There was nobody in my locker. The only thing that was there was the book.

I couldn't figure it out. I know what I heard, but I wasn't going to stay there alone trying to solve the mystery of the heavy breather for a second longer than I had to! I grabbed the book and hurried out of the storage facility.

I took the book to a dealer named Melinda Miller. She was a wiry woman with cotton ball hair who had to have been in her late 80's. I had consulted her for book appraisals many times in the past. She smoked like a chimney. Her habit cast a constant haze throughout her small vintage store which was wall to wall bookshelves. When I handed her the book she seemed impressed.

"This is ancient."

"Oh yeah? How ancient?"

Melinda studied the exterior of the book and ran her finger down the spine.

"At least fifteenth century."

My eyes widened.

"Fifteenth century?"

She nodded and glided her wrinkled hand over the title, which I was curious about.

"Do you have any idea what that says?"

"Mors est hic. It's Latin. Roughly translated it means…death is here."

That certainly coincided with the warning scribbled on the flyleaf. I was getting a bad feeling about all of this and it was obvious to Melinda that something was troubling me.

"What's wrong?"

"Take a look at the writing on the first page."

Melinda opened the immense book and smiled as she read the writing.

"I see someone was superstitious."

Fearless, she flipped past the warning to the next page and immediately I felt a cold chill fill the room. I felt the need to verify the temperature change.

"Is it just me or did it get chilly in here?"

Melinda held a smirk as she gazed in my direction.

"I see you're superstitious too. This store is drafty. Don't worry."

After dismissing the odd occurrence, Melinda squinted to read the text on the page. After a moment, she picked up a huge magnifying glass and held it close to the book. As she read silently, I swore I detected the same breathing sounds I'd heard back at Sam's Secure Storage.

"Do you hear that?"

Melinda reluctantly looked up from the book.

"Hear what?"

"Breathing! I heard someone else in this room, breathing."

"I told you, the store has a draft."

I shook my head.

"That was no draft."

She found my frightened state amusing and let out a chuckle as she spoke.

"Are you scared?"

I let out a deep breath, stuck out my chest and put on a brave face.

"Of course not. I'm not scared. I'm fine."

"You will be. Listen to the first line of the book."

Melinda held the magnifying glass to the page and read aloud.

"Death is in your future."

As the words passed by her lips, I felt a lanky hand come to rest on my right shoulder. I let out a yelp as I spun around only to see nobody.

Melinda looked up from the book.

"Are you alright?"

I was jittery as I spoke.

"Melinda, I have to go. I'll check back with you in the morning."

I rushed out of her store and didn't feel safe until I got home. I watched a few episodes of *Three's Company* to lighten the air and help me to relax and clear my mind of the darkness that seemed to surround that book.

The next morning I tried to call Melinda, but there was no answer, so I drove to her store. I was shocked to see an ambulance parked outside.

I bolted into the store. There sat Melinda in the same seat she was when I left, but she was drooped forward, face down within the open pages of the book.

The EMTs told me it was a heart attack. Due to Melinda's age and smoking habit, I probably would have believed them if I hadn't seen the pen in her dead hand. The point was still touching the note pad she had scrawled the following words on.

The book. Evil. Hide it.

Melinda had read the book and died just as it had warned.

I took the book to Sam's Secure Storage, rented the smallest, cheapest storage unit he had and locked the book inside.

Nobody will see that wicked thing again in my lifetime.

PINS AND NEEDLES

Am I the best husband in the world? Definitely not. But I'm a hell of a lot closer to the best than I am to the worst, I can tell you that.

I've never abused my wife in any way. I listen to her. I communicate fairly well. I'm rarely argumentative. I have never and would never cheat on her. Our sex life is reasonable. And I am financially successful.

Yet, Amy, my wife, has issues with me. Primarily that I work a lot. And she's correct. That is my biggest fault as far as our marriage goes.

It's not uncommon for me to get up in the morning, leave for work and not return home until close to bedtime. Weekends can get busy for me too if I allow it, but I always make sure that I take one full weekend day off to spend with my wife.

Her argument is that it's not enough.

I explained to her early in our relationship that I was a workaholic and my spare time was limited and she was okay with that. We dated for over a year before we got married. And I reminded her before we took our wedding vows that my schedule would remain the same, but she insisted she was fine with that.

Five years later, things have changed. My lack of time with her has taken its toll. Amy has become increasingly vocal about it. She says that she is lonely. I suppose that is why she has taken a lover.

That's right. She has been unfaithful.

The signs had been there the past few months. I noticed she was going out more often and making an effort to look especially attractive. She had been purchasing expensive undergarments, but wasn't wearing them in my presence. I noticed her texting on her phone much more than normal. Occasionally when I had extra time during the day, I'd try to reach out to her to see if she wanted to have lunch, but she would be unreachable.

I hired a private detective and he confirmed my suspicion. Amy was having an affair with her co-worker, Joel. They would get a hotel on their lunch breaks, typically on Mondays and Fridays. They'd have dinner together every Wednesday evening and then go back to his place.

It was around this time that I started having grueling lower abdominal cramps accompanied by paralyzing chest pains. It felt as though I were being stabbed with thousands of pins and needles! This was all brought on by stress, no doubt.

I stewed as I contemplated what my next action would be. I knew I wanted a divorce and I kept my private investigator on the job to gather as much incriminating evidence as he could to make sure I could break clean without having to pay alimony. If anything, I'd take *her* to the cleaners!

Over the next two weeks, the abdominal pains and the chest pains began to increase in intensity and frequency. I considered an emergency room stop on multiple occasions, but I was confident the prognosis would be stress related complications, so I opted to make an appointment with my regular doctor. Unfortunately, he didn't have an appointment available for two weeks, so I'd have to wait until then to hear him lecture me about reducing the stress in my life.

Then something interesting happened.

I decided to rummage through Amy's dresser drawers to see if I could find any evidence myself and came across something I wasn't expecting.

A doll.

It was a straw doll that had been dressed in snipped up fragments of my clothing. And the doll had enormous, intimidating pins sticking within the heart and stomach region of its anatomy.

Was this a damned voodoo doll?

It was then that I got a call from my private investigator. He informed me that he had collected enough intimate photographs of my wife and her lover to destroy her in divorce court.

The P.I. also shared another tidbit of information that I found intriguing. Amy had been frequenting a small store named, Bewitched. I paid a quick visit to the store and found that they provided everything that someone practicing voodoo could ever wish for.

Amy wasn't satisfied with cheating on me.

She wanted me dead.

I had to hand it to her, she had a solid plan. She'd gradually kill me allowing me ample time to complain of stomach and chest pains. When she finally ended my life people would be surprised, but say the warning signs were there. Then Amy would inherit everything.

She and Joel would live happily ever after.

I came home early from work one day and sat in the darkened corner of our bedroom. Amy entered the bedroom she didn't notice me. This wasn't surprising as I was never home at that time. I always worked late. That was my lone fault. The one that Amy thought I deserved to die for.

I watched for several minutes as she removed one of her favorite dresses from her closet and inspected it as if she noticed something wrong with the garment.

"I know about the affair."

Amy startled, but regained her composure quickly. She stood stoically and stared at me with an icy gaze. It was the look of a murderess.

"I have all the proof I need. You won't be getting one dime from me."

Amy smirked before she sprinted to the drawer to withdraw her secret weapon. She panicked and began rifling through the drawer when she couldn't find it.

"Looking for this?"

I held up the voodoo doll. The pins were gone and my clothing had been removed from it. When she recognized that the doll was now dressed in the fabric from her favorite dress, she gasped.

I didn't give her a chance to make any sudden moves or plea for mercy. I simply twisted the dolls head around and snapped it off.

MY DAUGHTER'S CREEPY DRAWINGS

I'm a single mother. When my 7 year old daughter, Lori's teacher called me in for an impromptu meeting, I was slightly concerned. I thought perhaps she was misbehaving or falling behind in class.

As it turns out, the teacher simply wanted to bring to my attention a picture that my daughter had drawn.

The picture was the kind of rudimentary, crayon drawing one may expect from a 7 year old. In the drawing was a smiling child with blonde hair. That was supposed to represent Lori. Lori was holding the hand of a tall woman with light blonde hair.

I'm short and have the blackest of black hair so the woman depicted in the drawing was certainly not me. Lori's teacher explained that when she asked Lori who the woman in the picture was, she said it was "The lady from my closet."

Lori's teacher and I both agreed this was likely nothing more than the overactive imagination of a 7 year old child. But she wanted to be sure just in case someone was interacting with Lori that I was unaware of.

We lived in a neighborhood that was exactly one block from Lori's school. The school was for students in kindergarten through 6th grade. All of the neighborhood kids walked to school together, including Lori. Several of the parents from the neighborhood made the trip too. I assumed the person Lori drew in the picture was one of the parents that walked them to school or perhaps one of the other teachers.

At dinner that night, I questioned little Lori about the drawing. When I asked her if it was someone that walked to school with the kids, she shook her head.

"Well, is it one of your teachers?"

Again, she shook her head, no.

"Who is the picture of, Lori?"

"It's me and the lady from my closet."

Actually hearing those words flow from my daughter's mouth sent a mild chill down my spine.

I told Lori to take me into her room and show me exactly where the woman came from. Not surprisingly, she led me to the small closet in her bedroom.

I opened the closet and peered about. There was nothing in there other than Lori's clothes and a few miscellaneous items stacked on the floor and on the shelf.

"I don't see her, sweetie. Where is she?"

"She only comes out at night, when I'm in bed."

I left it at that. I didn't want to push Lori any further on the subject. I was confident in my theory that it was just a matter of her imagination running wild, which was healthy.

The next day when I was cleaning Lori's room, I found another drawing. In this one, Lori was lying in bed and the tall woman with the light blond hair was sitting in a chair at the foot of the bed, watching Lori.

When Lori arrived home from school that day, I questioned her about the drawing.

"That's the lady from my closet. She watches over me when I sleep. She makes me promise that I will never leave her."

At this point, an imaginary friend seemed to make the most sense. My sister is a psychologist and I asked her about this behavior. She said that kids Lori's age having an imaginary friend is normal and can be beneficial.

Hearing that prognosis from my sister was a relief and made me feel much better. That is until the next day when I found another drawing.

The latest drawing was the most disturbing of all. It was another picture of Lori lying in bed. The tall woman was standing at the side of the bed and was holding a hatchet.

This troubled me to say the least.

As soon as Lori arrived from school I showed her the drawing and asked her about it.

"It's the lady from my closet."

"Why is she holding a hatchet?"

"She's protecting me. The woman from my closet says that if anyone tries to hurt me, she'll chop their heads off."

The next day I scheduled a meeting to talk to Lori's teachers and the principal. I wanted to find out if they noticed any evidence of abnormal behavior from Lori, so I got the teenage girl from next door to babysit Lori until I returned home.

All of those who interacted with Lori daily stated that Lori was behaving the same as always and was excelling in all areas, academically and socially.

When I showed them the picture, they were as concerned as I was.

"Lori's name for this woman is unnerving. She calls her, the lady from my closet."

Lori's principal thought a moment.

"Where do you live?"

"Right over on Lotus Drive."

"What's your exact address?"

"130 Lotus Drive."

The room fell silent for a long moment. I started looking around, confused.

"What?"

The principal directed his next question at Lori's teacher.

"How long ago was it when you saw Lori's first drawing that depicted the tall woman in it?"

"About a week ago."

The principal stared into space for a moment as he thought and a worried expression washed over his face.

"Dear God."

I stood up.

"What? Tell me what is going on!"

"Five years ago, one of the most tragic events in our small town took place. A woman named Jill Harlow, who was recently divorced, lost custody of her twin daughters. She had a complete mental breakdown and chopped her daughters up with a hatchet. Written in their blood on the wall were the words, I couldn't let them leave me. They found the dead bodies, but couldn't find Jill. Weeks went by and they finally picked her up at a local grocery store."

The gruesome story had me sick to my stomach, but I couldn't understand why the principal was telling me all of this.

"What does this have to do with Lori?"

"Jill Harlow lived at 130 Lotus Drive."

"Well, where is she now?"

"For the past five years she has resided at the Paducah Valley Insane Asylum. That was until a week ago when she escaped. They have yet to find her."

My eyes widened in fear.

"Call the police!"

The words hadn't fully left my mouth before I was racing out of the school and into my car. I floored it home and came to a skidding halt in my driveway. I bolted into my house and was weakened in the knees by the stench of death and the ghastly sight before me.

The babysitter had been hacked to bits. Parts of her body and blood were splattered all over the room.

"Mommy!"

Lori's tormented cry was coming from her bedroom.

I raced into her room, but didn't see Lori anywhere!

"Lori! Lori, where are you?"

"Mommy!"

Her voice was coming from the closet.

I flung the closet door open, but she wasn't there! I shoved her clothes aside as I rummaged through the closet searching for my daughter!

"Mommy, help me!"

Lori's cries of help were coming from under the closet!

That's when I noticed the edge of the carpet toward the back of the closet was propped up. I instantly ripped it back to reveal a wooden trapdoor in the floor. I pulled the trapdoor open and found a small ladder that dropped down approximately six feet into the earth.

I flew down the ladder and found myself in a small dirt room. Empty water bottles and food containers littered the room. I noticed a bundle of blankets and a pillow in one of the corners.

"She's mine! You can't have her!"

I spun around at the sound of the crazed woman's demented voice. Jill Harlow's long, messy blond hair was covering the majority of her face, but I could see her psychopathic eyes darting back and forth from me to Lori!

Lori was lying on the dirty ground. Jill Harlow was standing over her holding a hatchet in the air.

"If I can't have her, nobody can!"

Jill Harlow made a motion as if she were going to bring the hatchet down and bury it into my helpless daughter! I let out a war cry as I rushed her and she attempted to turn the weapon on me, but I was able to slam her against the wall before she could swing it.

The hatchet went sprawling across the primitive room. I tried to crawl to it, but the tall woman pulled me by my leg and started pounding on me relentlessly. I was on the verge of losing consciousness when the room echoed with gunfire.

Jill Harlow fell to the ground in a lifeless heap, full of a policeman's bullets. I cradled Lori in my arms until the EMTs arrived on the scene.

The secret room under the closet was where Jill Harlow hid from police after she murdered her daughters. When she escaped from the insane asylum, she sought refuge there once again.

Lori and I were both fine physically, just a few scratches here and there. But psychologically, I'm not sure if either of us will ever fully recover.

DON'T GO INTO THE HOUSE
Herbert

I hated Lonnie.

I was 10. He was 11. I was in 5th grade. He was in 6th grade. And he was mean. He picked on me any time he saw me. He'd knock the books out of my hands, trip me in the cafeteria and make me spill my food tray, push me to the ground, call me names and sometimes he'd make me give him my lunch money.

Lonnie lived in my neighborhood and we had the same bus stop. So even if I didn't see him during school, I'd always see him before and after school. There was no escape from him.

The only thing that scared me more than Lonnie was the Marlowe house. It was the biggest house on the street and nobody had ever lived there as far as I knew.

The house was three stories tall and was falling apart. There was a bunch of shingles missing from the roof. The siding on the house was old gray wood and some of the wood pieces were gone or dangling by a nail. The top two windows on the 3rd floor looked like evil eyes staring over the neighborhood. The long covered porch looked like a big, nasty mouth. The porch rails looked like teeth. I always thought it looked like the house was snarling at me.

One day I was walking past the Marlowe house. Lonnie was walking behind me as was a big girl from his grade named Bailey. Lonnie could tell I was scared of the house and started teasing me about it.

As we were passing by the house Lonnie came to a halt and told me that if I didn't stop too that meant I was a chicken. I guess I wanted to impress him. Maybe if he thought I was brave he'd stop picking on me so much. So I stopped. Bailey did also.

All three of us gawked at it. It was the spookiest house I had ever seen. I was certain I saw one of the curtains of the 2nd floor windows move! I wanted to run so bad, but I knew that Lonnie would make fun of me and never let me hear the end of it, so I stood there staring at the Marlowe house waiting for Lonnie to get tired of this charade and allow us to start walking again. Instead, he upped the ante.

"Walk up to the front door, Herbert."

I looked at him. My eyes were swimming with fright and he recognized it. My fear was like blood in the water for Lonnie. He grinned and pointed at the Marlowe house.

"Go on, you chicken shit!"

I jumped at his sharp tone. I didn't want to do it, but the fear of Lonnie's torment had me taking steps toward the dreaded house. I fixed my eyes on the front door. It was solid wood and appeared to be rotten in spots. When I reached the porch stairs, I stopped and looked back at Lonnie, hoping that would be good enough.

"Hurry up! I don't have all damn day!"

I took a deep breath and began walking up the steps. Each step let out a hideous creak when I put weight on them. And just like that I was on the porch standing near the front door.

Oddly enough, I felt a surge of pride rush through my body. I did it. I actually found the courage to walk right up to the front door of the house I feared more than anything. I think I was grinning when I looked back at Lonnie for approval. Unfortunately, he wasn't impressed.

"Now go inside!"

I instantly began shaking my head. This angered Lonnie.

"Go inside right now or I'm going to kick your ass! Do you hear me?"

My entire body began to tremble for I knew I had to do it. Lonnie wasn't bluffing. He would add daily beatings to the schedule if I didn't.

I turned and faced the door. I took in a deep breath and reached for the rusty doorknob. Just as my skin brushed against the knob I felt a gust of wind at my back and the front door creaked open on its own.

It was just the wind that opened the door. It was just the wind. It wasn't a ghost. I kept repeating those thoughts in my mind as I took my first few steps into the Marlowe house.

The house was dirty and covered in cobwebs. The floor had big rotten holes in some sections. I was afraid if I walked too fast, I may fall through the floor, so I took slow, careful steps toward the staircase that dominated the front room.

I was deep enough in the house that I was no longer in Lonnie's sight. My plan was to just stand there for a few minutes and then go back out. If I could do that, Lonnie would have a newfound respect for me even if he would never admit it.

My plan was to count to ninety and then bravely step out onto the porch. If I could remember to, I'd shrug as if the whole thing was no big deal, even though my heart was beating out of my chest and I was shaking with fear.

When I reached seventy, I heard soft footsteps walking around upstairs. And they were getting louder and closer. I could tell they had reached the top of the staircase.

I wasn't alone! I about peed my pants when I heard the voice.

"Get your ass out of here or die!"

I darted out of the house, down the porch stairs and right past Lonnie. He yelled out something insulting as I ran down the street, but I didn't care. I didn't stop running until I got home.

DON'T GO INTO THE HOUSE
Bailey

My name is Bailey. I'm on the large side. Some might call me obese. Others may call me fat. But they'd only call me fat one time. After I beat the hell out of them, they'd never call me fat again. As a matter of fact, nobody had called me fat in years. My reputation preceded me.

I was 11 and in the same grade as Lonnie. Lonnie was the biggest jerk at our school. He picked on any kids smaller than him. He was also a tyrant within the neighborhood too. He egged houses and broke windows among other forms of childish vandalism.

Fortunately, he wasn't in any of my classes so I didn't have to put up with him in school. But I did share a bus stop with the jerk, so I had to experience him before and after school.

Let me make it clear, Lonnie never picked on me. I'd beat him up if he did and he knew it. Getting his ass kicked by a girl would make him a laughingstock so he steered clear of me. But he picked on poor little Herbert, relentlessly.

The latest tactic was daring Herbert to go up to the front porch of the Marlowe house, something I had never seen any kid do before.

The Marlowe house was haunted. I walked past that house twice a day for the past five years. I've seen shadows move across the curtains. I've heard doors shutting. I've seen the front door open all by itself and I've heard voices coming from inside.

Everybody was scared of that place. I was proud of little Herbert for having the guts to walk right up to that door. I was about to applaud him when stupid Lonnie yelled out "Now go inside!"

Lonnie demanded that Herbert go into the house or he'd beat him up. It wasn't fair. Of course Herbert wasn't going to go inside. Lonnie knew that. This was just an excuse for him to bully Herbert even more.

When Herbert opened the door and stepped inside, I let out a gasp. I looked over at Lonnie. His jaw dropped open so much it was practically touching the ground!

At that point, Herbert was a legend. There was nothing Lonnie could do about it. The deed had been done. Herbert was inside the haunted Marlowe house and we anxiously awaited his return.

We were both getting nervous for Herbert with each passing second. I was starting to fidget and I could hear the nervousness in Lonnie's voice when he said, "Boy, he's been in there a long time."

It was then that Herbert came barreling out of the house as if he had just seen a ghost. He rushed right past me and Lonnie and down the road. Lonnie laughed and yelled out at him.

"Herbert, you pussy!"

Lonnie stood cackling for a few seconds. In his simple mind, everything Herbert had just accomplished was null and void because he ran out of the house scared. That was nonsense and I called Lonnie out on his bullshit.

"You go inside."

His laughter immediately stopped and he took on a serious expression.

"What?"

"Little Herbert had the balls to go inside the haunted Marlowe house. Now let's see you do it."

Lonnie started to stammer as he tried to come up with an excuse against going inside the intimidating house, but he had no words.

"Go ahead Lonnie. Go in. Or are *you* the pussy?"

He shook his head.

"I'm not a pussy. I'm not scared to go in there."

"Then do it!"

Lonnie was growing more nervous by the second as he started looking back and forth from the Marlowe house to me, so I decided to give him some extra incentive.

"If you don't go inside the house, I'm going to tell everyone at school tomorrow that little Herbert was brave enough to go in but you were nothing but a chicken shit! Bawk, bawk, bawk, bawk, bawk!"

My chicken noises pushed Lonnie over the edge and he lashed out at me defiantly.

"All right! Fine! I'll do it!"

Lonnie took in a deep breath before he marched right up to the front door. Then his fear visibly kicked in. I could see his hand shaking as he reached out for the doorknob and then pulled his hand away. I thought that was a good moment to give him a dose of his own medicine.

"Go in! Hurry up! I don't have all damn day!"

Lonnie stared daggers at me, but he knew he had to go through with it. He'd never live it down otherwise, so he actually impressed me by turning the doorknob, pushing the door open and stepping into the house.

It was five minutes later when I heard him scream.

DON'T GO INTO THE HOUSE
Old Man Travis

Everyone in the neighborhood calls me Old Man Travis. I've been here longer than anyone.

I live next door to the Marlowe house.

Not many people know this, but I was the last person to live in the Marlowe house. It's been vacant ever since.

Some claim that the Marlowe house is haunted and those people are correct. Nobody is more aware of that fact than I am.

It was back in the early 1980's when I bought the house. Back then, my wife was still alive and the Marlowe house was in good condition. It wasn't the eyesore that it is today.

From day one, the house didn't want us there and it wasn't shy about letting us know. At first it tried to scare us away by slamming doors before we could enter a room. When that didn't work it spoke to us in a demonic sounding voice.

"Get out!"

My wife and I were both stubborn. I suppose that's what drew us together. In this case however, our stubbornness did not do us any favors. Late one night when my wife was heading to our bedroom, the door slammed shut and she felt a legion of hands grab her by the arms, drag her to the staircase and shove her down.

She broke both of her legs.

It was then that we conceded and left the house. But we didn't want to leave the area.

So, I spoke to the Marlowe house.

We owned the property all around the house. I told it that if it allowed us to build a small cottage next door and let us live there in peace, we'd make sure the Marlowe house stayed vacant. I even told it that I would keep the yard in check so that it didn't overtake the house and that I'd keep trespassers at bay.

When I felt the reassuring pat of multiple unseen hands on my back, I knew we had a deal and I've kept my end of the bargain ever since. If any neighborhood brat was stupid enough to try to enter the house, I'd scare them away. Luckily, I didn't have to do that very often. Most people were so scared of the house they didn't want anything to do with it.

When I saw that little asshole Lonnie, daring poor little Herbert to go into the house, I knew I had to do something to frighten them away. I hurried around the back of the Marlowe house and snuck in through the fruit cellar. I then made my way upstairs and waited.

Poor little Herbert. I could see that he was trembling like a leaf. It wouldn't take much to scare him away, so I cupped my hands around my mouth and growled out, "Get your ass out of here or die!"

That kid might have pissed his pants! I never saw someone run so fast!

I was laughing when I peered through the window and saw the other two kids still standing there.

Why hadn't they left too?

I could see the plump girl motioning to the house daring Lonnie to go inside. It took some coaxing, but the little jerk finally did it.

Lonnie was a menace to the neighborhood. He had egged my house and broke one of my windows. On Halloween he lit a sack of dog crap on fire and set it in front of my front door. As if anyone falls for that old trick anymore.

Yeah, it was going to be a real pleasure to scare the hell out of that jerk of a kid.

I watched Lonnie when he got inside the house. He was scared, but had a determination about him. And unlike little Herbert, he didn't just step inside the house and stand still. Lonnie was venturing through the house and found his way upstairs.

I had a classic Tor Johnson latex mask that I pulled out for occasions such as this. I put it on and hid inside of one of the upstairs bedrooms. I could hear Lonnie's footsteps getting closer and closer and finally, at the perfect moment, I leapt out in front of the little tyke and let forth with a monstrous bellow!

Lonnie let out a loud scream! He was white as a ghost as he turned, ran and then stumbled. He fell hard down the staircase.

I walked to the top of the staircase and looked down at Lonnie. He was lying still. I didn't even have to inspect him to be sure if he was okay or not. I could clearly see that his head was twisted all the way around.

He was dead.

I peeked out the window and crossed my fingers that the plump girl wouldn't come in looking for him. I was relieved when she waved Lonnie and the house off and walked away.

She didn't care about Lonnie. Nobody did. He was a menace and the neighborhood would be better off without him.

I left Lonnie's dead body lying at the foot of the staircase and went home.

I knew I wouldn't have to tend to the body. The Marlowe house would take care of that. It always did. I don't know what it did with the dead bodies when this kind of thing happened. All I know is there's never any trace of them the next day.

EAVESDROPPING ON MY NEIGHBOR

I live a quiet life. I work at a print shop from 9am to 6pm, Monday thru Friday. I come home, make dinner and read until it's time to go to bed.

On weekends I spice my routine up a bit. I get up, read and then treat myself to a restaurant dinner. After that, I come back home and read until bedtime.

If you haven't guessed yet, I'm an avid reader. I don't even own a television set. I don't need one. Reading is all the entertainment that I need.

One night as I returned home from work, I was considering which new book to start when I saw her. She was tall, lean and had the most beautiful, wavy golden hair. She appeared to be in her early 30's which made her age compatible with me. She was balancing two large cardboard boxes on her knee as she tried to unlock the door to the apartment next door to mine.

That apartment was the last one at the end of the hall. It had sat empty since I had moved in last year.

I hurried to her aid and grabbed the boxes.

"Let me help you out."

The woman's smile was breathtaking.

"You're a lifesaver!"

She unlocked her door and pushed it open.

"I guess we're neighbors. My name is Trish."

I would have shaken her hand, but I was holding the boxes, so I just nodded politely.

"I'm Henry. Welcome to the building."

Trish took the boxes from me and gave me a departing smile before disappearing into her apartment. But not before I was able to sneak a peek at her hands and recognize that she was without a wedding ring.

Thoughts of Trish and everything else blew away once I opened up the first page of the new book. That's what reading did for me. It allowed me to forget all about the few cares I had and to disappear into another world.

The book was good and my mind was deeply entrenched when I heard a feminine voice coming from the corner of the room. I lowered my book and my ears perked up when I heard it again. It was coming from the wall I shared with the new tenant I had just met, Trish.

The walls within the apartment complex were unexpectedly thick, so I was surprised I could hear her. As I listened on for several minutes, I quickly determined that I could only hear her if she were talking near the far corner of the wall. If she were anywhere else, I couldn't hear a peep from her.

The rest of the night and following week, I didn't hear anything else coming from her side of the wall and I forgot all about it until the next time I saw Trish. We were both entering our apartments at the same time. She shot me a friendly smile and I found myself getting lost in her hypnotic blue eyes. I grinned goofily and gave her a quick wave.

"Howdy neighbor."

I made a point to look at her hands again. Yep, definitely no ring!

That night, I was nearing the end of another book when I heard Trish's unmistakable, high pitched, harmonious voice. At first it started out as an inaudible mumble, but then she stepped near the sweet spot in the wall and I could hear her words.

I jumped up, hurried to the wall and pressed my ear against it. I could make out what she said as if I were standing in the room with her.

"He lives in the apartment right next to mine. He's very good looking. I think he's single too. I didn't see a ring."

After that she stepped away from the wall and her enchanting voice transitioned into a mumble and then silence.

Very good looking? Me? Wow. I wasn't expecting that! Don't get me wrong. I'm not a bad looking guy. I'm of average height and build and I wear glasses, but I get compliments on my curly, black hair and dimples.

I wasn't much in the way of a ladies man. As a matter of fact, I hadn't had a girlfriend in many years, so I wasn't sure how to proceed. Should I ask her out on a date or would that be too forward? Maybe just play it cool and see where simple chit chat leads us?

That seemed easy and safe, so I went with that strategy. The problem was, we didn't run into each other often. But nonetheless, I opted for patience.

It was a week later when I checked my mail and found a letter in there addressed to Trish Stratton. I had received a piece of her mail by mistake! This was the perfect opportunity to knock on her door and see her. Who knows, maybe she'd invite me in and things would skyrocket from there!

I waited until I knew she was home, ate a dinner mint and headed to her apartment with her mail in hand. I cleared my throat, took in a deep breath and knocked. She answered quickly and grinned. I could see in her heavenly eyes that she was confused as to why I was there, so I quickly held up the letter.

"I think I received a piece of your mail by mistake."

Her smile widened enough to show off those dazzling white teeth.

"Oh, thanks!"

She took the letter from me and took a step back.

"Have a nice night."

With that, she closed the door.

Not the response I was hoping for, but it was still a polite, friendly interaction. Maybe enough such exchanges would lead to more conversation which may lead to something significant.

Slow and steady wins the race.

As usual, I escaped into a book that night. I was so lost in the book I initially tuned out Trish's voice when I heard her near the wall, but I quickly withdrew myself from the world of the book and rushed to the wall to hear her better. Her dainty voice was intoxicating. I was hopeful that she would mention me again.

To my chagrin, she did.

"Turns out the guy who lives next door, is a total creep..."

Her words trailed off as she walked away from the wall and my heart dropped to the floor.

Creep? Me?

All I did was hand her some mail that had found its way into my mailbox. Did she think I stole it or something along those lines? I didn't understand. I wasn't guilty of anything that should have elevated me to creep status.

I was perplexed.

For the next few days, I couldn't concentrate on work, I couldn't focus on reading, I was obsessed with finding out the reason Trish was seemingly so down on me. I was driving myself mad just sitting around pondering what I had done wrong, so I decided to take the initiative. One way or the other, I was going to find out what the issue was. I was going to march over to Trish's apartment and ask her out for drinks. When she declined, I could flat out ask her if I did something wrong and hopefully get to the bottom of all this.

I was nervous when I stepped in front of the door, but I didn't let that deter me. I knocked confidently and only had to wait a few seconds before the door swung open. Trish's eyes had a sparkle in them and her smile was welcoming. She didn't look at me like she thought I was a creep.

"Hi Trish, listen I was wondering if you'd like to go out for a drink sometime."

I was surprised when she smiled giddily and was shocked by her answer.

"I'd love to! But I'm tied up for the next several nights. Maybe in a week or two?"

I nodded.

"Sounds good."

I walked back to my apartment in a confused state.

Had she just accepted my date proposal or was that the nicest I had ever been blown off? I wasn't quite sure.

I went back to my apartment and sat down while my mind swam around in a river of possibilities. Maybe she really wanted to go out for drinks. Maybe it was that simple. Or maybe putting it off for a week or two was her way of saying no, in hopes that I'd get the hint and leave it be.

When I heard her voice by the wall, I walked over, listened and got my answer.

"The guy next door is starting to scare me. I don't know what I should do."

Scaring her? I was scaring her? Seriously? By asking her out on a date? This woman must have a screw loose.

It took me a couple hours of juggling the absurdity of her being frightened by me to finally lay it all to rest. If she thought I was creepy and was scared of me, fine. I wouldn't talk to her and that would be that.

And that's the way it was. I went back to my regular, mundane life of working and reading and forgot all about Trish Stratton.

That is until one night when I heard her angelic voice as I was stepping into my apartment.

"Hey, Henry!"

I stopped and gawked her way. She was walking down the hall toward me. She seemed very sociable and cheerful.

"We should do those drinks soon. How about Friday?"

Wait. What? Did she just make a date with me? But I'm a creep. She's scared of me. Why would she want to make a date with me?

I found myself nodding.

"Yes."

Her eyes twinkled with delight.

"Great! Then it's a date."

I watched her until she went into her apartment and closed the door behind her.

What was going on with this girl? One second she's scared of me, the next she's happy to see me and wanting to go out for drinks?

I stepped into my apartment. My mind was whirling in confusion. When I heard her talking near the sweet spot in the wall, I rushed over in hopes of hearing some clarification. And clarification I got.

"I'm going to kill him. I'm going to poison his drink..."

Her voice transitioned into a mumble as she walked away from the wall.

Now it all made sense. No wonder she was acting so charming and wanted to make a date for drinks. She was planning on murdering me!

I wasn't sure what to do. A normal person may take this information and go to the police, but I couldn't do that.

You see, there's something about me that I didn't mention. When I was a senior in high school, my girlfriend broke up with me. It was unexpected and I guess I went a little crazy.

I snuck into her house late one night, went into her bedroom and smothered her to death with a pillow.

I instantly regretted it, but the act had already been committed. It wasn't going to take Sherlock Holmes to figure out who the murderer was. The way I figured it, I had an eight to twelve hour window before anyone found out, so I drove and drove until I found myself more than halfway across the country in some little town I had no ties to.

I spent a week hiding in a hotel and drastically changed my appearance from a straight haired red head who wore contacts to a curly, black haired guy with eye glasses. I spent a pretty penny getting a fake social security number and driver's license. And just like that, I had a new identity.

I live a very quiet, simple life. I keep to myself. I don't ruffle anyone's feathers. And I never, under any circumstances, go to the police for anything, including when I know the woman next door is going to kill me.

No. This was something I was going to have to handle myself.

I murdered before. I could murder again.

I waited until after midnight and quietly knocked on her door. It took a few minutes but she finally answered. Her lovely hair was slightly ruffled and she was wearing a night shirt.

I gave her no time to make a sound. I slapped my hand over her mouth and pushed her into her apartment. She stumbled backwards, tripped over her own feet and fell onto her back which made things even easier for me.

I kept one hand over her mouth to muffle her screams and wrapped my other hand around her throat and squeezed the life out of her. She died quickly without any complications.

Now it was just a matter of getting rid of the body. But that would be easy. I'd put her in her bathtub, cut her up into enough pieces to fit into one or two of her suitcases and toss them in a nearby river.

I leaned my back against the wall and took in several calming breaths as I stared at the gorgeous woman and shook my head.

"It didn't have to be this way."

My gaze shifted from Trish's dead body to a book that was sitting on her coffee table that had a book mark in it. Apparently Trish was a reader too. Such a shame. We shared my only real interest. Too bad she was a murderous psycho.

I was curious as to what she was reading, so I picked up the book and looked at the cover. It wasn't a novel. It was a stage play. The title was *I Killed My Neighbor.*

I opened to the first page and noticed that there was a cast list. Trish Stratton's name was at the top of the list. She was cast in the role of "Nelda, the murderess."

I flipped through the pages of the script and saw that Trish had highlighted all of the lines for the character she was playing. I read one of the lines.

He lives in the apartment right next to mine. He's very good looking. I think he's single too. I didn't see a ring.

That line. That was the first thing I ever heard Trish say through the wall!

I leafed through more pages and my heart sank as I spotted several familiar lines.

Turns out the guy who lives next door is a total creep.
The guy next door is starting to scare me. I don't know what I should do.
I'm going to kill him. I'm going to poison his drink.

Trish was an actress who was doing nothing more than rehearsing for a stage play. Our interactions were genuine. She was truly interested in having drinks and getting to know me. Who knows where our relationship could have led.

I disposed of the body with no issues. There were a few inquiries as to Trish Stratton's whereabouts, but no one even questioned me, since I didn't really know her. Hell, I'm not sure they even suspected foul play.

I try not to think about it much. Losing myself in a book every night helps, but I can't lie. This one hurts.

THE GLOP

I found myself fidgeting and jiggling my car keys within my pocket as I waited in line at the bank. I didn't have time for this, but I needed some cash. My car was on empty, the only gas station in town's credit card machine was broken and the bank's ATM was down.

When I heard the car alarm going off, I didn't think much of it. We all hear those pesky alarms every day and tend to zone them out since they typically are turned off within a few alarm honks.

After a solid two minutes, everyone in the bank was growing frustrated and looking around, hoping the guilty party would shut off the annoying alarm. I was doing the same thing.

When I peered out into the bank parking lot, I could see the flashing lights of the car in question as the alarm continued to blare and quickly realized it was my car! I must have hit the panic button on my keys when I was jiggling them around in my pocket!

I removed my keys from my pocket and hit the panic button. That did nothing to halt the irritating alarm so I hit the unlock button multiple times and finally the alarm stopped. A few people in the bank applauded. I didn't blame them.

Once I finished my transaction, I hurried out to my car and immediately became concerned when I noticed that the back door was ajar.

"Oh no."

I rushed to my vehicle and my worst fear was realized. The cage sitting in my back seat was empty.

"Oh no!"

It must have gotten out of the cage and when I unlocked the doors to turn off that damned alarm, it allowed it to open the car door and escape.

"No, please no."

I gazed about at the surrounding area and saw no signs of it. This was bad. This was really, really bad.

My name is Larry Jenson. I'm a curator for a rather unique museum called The Crypto Zoo. It focuses on cryptozoological exhibits.

We have entire displays dedicated to the most famous cryptids such as Sasquatch, The Loch Ness Monster, Mothman, El Chupacabra, The Jersey Devil, Mermaids, The Beast of Exmoor, The Michigan Dog Man and the Florida Skunk Ape among others.

The one thing The Crypto Zoo was missing was a live exhibit, but that was all about to change.

I got a call from a colleague of mine located in the southwest who claimed to have captured an obscure cryptid in his area simply referred to as, The Glop.

The Glop was a giant form of gastropod, more commonly known as snails or slugs. But it differed from gastropods by having a mouth equipped with razor-like teeth and an aggressive nature. Also, it could supposedly slither around at speeds upwards of 20 miles per hour.

When I was told he caught one, I have to admit I wasn't expecting anything other than an abnormally large slug, but that wasn't the case at all.

First of all, it was the size of a large beagle. Secondly, it had a distinct snout, similar to a wolf and its sharp teeth were visible. Its head was similar to a snail, but its antennae-like tentacles atop its head had suction cups on it not unlike an octopus and its pronounced eyes at the end of each tentacle gave me the impression that this creature could see quite well. Its slimy body did have a shell, but not like a snail, it was more like the exoskeleton of a beetle.

The Glop was both fascinating and terrifying.

My colleague had The Glop trapped in a modest size dog cage. He assured me that it was slow like a normal slug and had not shown any aggressive tendencies as the legend claimed. Evidently he found it in the depths of a cold, cave hidden on the edge of the sleepy little town I found myself in.

The Glop was going to be the first live exhibit at The Crypto Zoo and would put us on the map!

I put the cage in the back of my car and began my journey back home. I immediately noticed that once in my car, The Glop became much more active. It began wriggling back and forth in the cage and continued to wrap its tentacles around the cage bars.

My colleague insisted that The Glop was lethargic, but it appeared it was becoming more energetic as it got warmer.

I didn't think it had the intelligence to open the cage door, but evidently it did. And when I inadvertently unlocked my car to turn the annoying alarm off, it allowed The Glop to open the car door and escape.

The creature was much cleverer than I had anticipated. And now it was gone! My prized possession that would turn The Crypto Zoo into a worldwide attraction was on the loose.

When I heard a loud scream emanating from the back of a fast food restaurant located one parking lot over from the bank, I had high hopes that someone spotted The Glop and that I could retrieve it!

I quickly pulled my .38 revolver from my glove compartment and raced to the back of the restaurant where I found a female employee in her early 20's, wearing an apron and grasping at her arm. I could see blood oozing from between her fingers.

"What happened?"

"Some kind of slimy monster bit me!"

It was The Glop. The characteristic of it being aggressive was clearly true. I could only surmise that the warmer it got the more aggressive and savage it became.

I followed the screech of tires and loud crash of cars colliding. I had to assume The Glop was responsible somehow. When I arrived at the crash site, I saw The Glop plastered on the windshield of a car. Its tentacle was balled up like a fist and in one motion it shattered the windshield and then slid its tentacle inside the car and wrapped it around the driver.

The beast had no problem extracting the person through the broken windshield and then it proceeded to wrap its monstrosity of a mouth around the individual's head and bite it off with ease.

"No!"

Somehow this monster had lived in the cold caves of the region far away from people. The cool environment obviously kept its temperament in check. And now I had released it upon the population in its most diabolic, invasive form.

I had to stop it!

I took a wild shot at it but missed. The Glop was aware that I was trying to kill it and fled. I chased it through the streets, but it was much faster than me. However, even though I couldn't catch it, I spotted it slinking into a darkened alley in the heart of town.

This was my chance.

I slowed when I reached the alley entrance and took a quick glance down it. The alley was lined with dumpsters. The rotting stench of garbage was strong in the air. I practically had to hold my breath as I began my journey down the alleyway.

I didn't spot The Glop, but began following the unusual, wet, slimy suction sounds that were stemming from a darkened, filthy corner of the alley.

"Holy shit."

I was both shocked and aghast at the sight before me! The Glop was ripping itself into two pieces. Once that act was complete, one half of The Glop slid on top of its other half.

It took me a moment to realize that this was a form of fission similar to a reproduction measure used by starfish. The Glop had split itself into two organisms and was currently in the act of breeding!

I lifted my revolver, aimed and pulled the trigger. I hit the creature that was on top of the other one. It splattered into black, bloody chunks against the brick wall behind it.

The second half of the creature let out a squeal and slithered up the side of the wall at a blinding speed. I squeezed two shots off at it, but I missed and The Glop scurried away onto the roof of a building.

I spent the rest of the night searching for The Glop but never found it. I did however find dozens of clear, gelatinous egg clusters stuck on the side of buildings, cars, trees, road signs…they were everywhere and they were hatching.

The reproduction capabilities of The Glop were out of this world. I could only theorize that the number of offspring would depend on the creature's food availability as is the case with fast breeding snail species. To The Glop, the world likely looks like an endless food buffet so I expect an uncontrollable population explosion which will likely end the world as we know it.

I knew the creature's weakness was cold temperatures, but it appeared that the mindboggling rate at which The Glop could multiply would render that knowledge meaningless.

I like to think that The Glop would have found its way out of the cold cave it lived in and that this result was inevitable. But the fact is that this monster finding its way into our world is my fault.

I guess the silver lining is that I won't have to live with the guilt for too long.

BLOOD SPORT

My name is Marty. I was the 3rd string wide receiver on the high school football team. I didn't play much. Our offense ran more than it passed and on passing downs our quarterback usually targeted the #1 wide receiver on the team, Devin Brown. When he wasn't open, he'd look for the #2 receiver, Les Tolbert.

I hardly ever got on the field. That is until our #1 receiver, Devin Brown went missing.

One day he didn't show up for practice after school. He never went home either. He was just gone.

Devin was a nice kid. He got along with everyone. He wasn't just a good football player, he was also a straight A student. And according to his parents he was a model son. He never got into trouble or did anything wrong.

Devin Brown simply vanished without a trace. The police had no leads. There were no clues. It was a mystery.

But life went on. And so did football. Les Tolbert took over the #1 wide receiver duties and I stepped up to #2. Suddenly I was on the field a lot more and the QB would occasionally throw me the ball.

After a couple of weeks, I was really settling into my #2 wide receiver role when something strange happened.

Les Tolbert went missing.

This was the same situation as Devin Brown. He was absent from school one day. He didn't show up to practice. He didn't make it home. He just disappeared.

Unlike Devin, Les wasn't a great student. He did just well enough to stay on the football team. He was also a bit of a ruffian. He had a short temper and got into a lot of fights at school. I also heard he liked to drink on weekends after the games, but I never saw it myself.

Again, the police had no answers. There were no clues. Nobody was coming forward with any suggestions or evidence.

As the mystery of the missing players continued to grow, I found myself benefiting from it. I was now the #1 wide receiver on the team.

With our top two receivers gone, the offense shifted to a purely running attack. I was used less at the new #1 wide receiver than I was when I was the #2 wide receiver. Now the offense was centered on our star running back, Bud Bryant.

It was the right decision. Bud was a brute. He was built low to the ground and was stocky and thick. He was a monster to tackle.

I was on the field a lot, I just helped block for Bud. I didn't have many balls thrown my way. That is, until Bud Bryant went missing. And when Bud went missing there was evidence.

Blood.

They found a smear of blood on the ground near the spot that Bud always parked his car.

The police questioned everybody who knew Bud, including all the members of the team, but a week later they had not made any progress.

And I continued to profit.

With the top two wide receivers and the star running back all gone, I became a focal point of the offense. Balls were being thrown my way consistently. I was catching the passes and racking up yards. I was faster and better than ever! I was thriving.

And I was feeling guilty.

It didn't feel right that I was benefiting from my teammates being gone due to potential nefarious circumstances. I wasn't sleeping well. I couldn't concentrate. I had to do something about it. So I decided to start looking into the disappearances of my teammates, myself.

The first thing I did was hone in on the one person, other than me, who was benefitting from the other players going missing.

Tanner Cornwall. He was the backup running back. With the #1 and #2 receivers gone, we became even more of a running team. With our star running back gone, Tanner became the bell cow. Even though I was benefiting, it wasn't as much as Tanner was.

Tanner was my #1 suspect, so I began following him.

He spent a lot of his time sitting on a bench overlooking a large lake that was near my home. More interesting was the fact that he was spending a considerable amount of time with Devin Brown's grieving girlfriend.

He was courting her.

Tanner was benefitting from the players going missing in more ways than one!

I went back and forth as to whether or not I should question Tanner. Eventually I came to the conclusion that I would have a difficult time living with myself if I didn't go the distance and do everything I could to find out the truth.

I waited one night after practice when Tanner and I were the only ones left on the field. We were the star players now and were putting in the extra work to be all that we could be.

I started the conversation by stating the obvious.

"We're both really taking advantage of the others not being here, aren't we?"

Tanner gave me a hefty stare before he spoke.

"Yeah. Sure."

I moved closer to Tanner and got to the point.

"Do you remember the last time you saw Bud?"

Tanner quickly became agitated.

"Shut up, Marty!"

It was time to call him out.

"It was you, Tanner. Wasn't it? You did it."

Tanner gave me a shove.

"I didn't do anything other than keep my mouth shut!"

He knew something and I was confident that the more I prodded him, the more he would talk.

"Tell me, Tanner. Tell me everything you know!"

"What? Like how you used to be a slow lethargic receiver until recently?"

"We're not talking about me, Tanner. We're talking about you."

"How'd you get so fast, Marty? Why are you suddenly such a better player than you used to be?"

"Stop changing the subject and confess! You killed them, didn't you? You killed them all!"

Tanner spent a few seconds staring at me while holding a bewildered expression.

"What are you talking about, Marty? *You* killed them."

My eyes crinkled in confusion. What was Tanner's game? What was he trying to accomplish? I listened intently as he continued.

"I was in the locker room the day the coach chewed you out for being slow and lazy. You didn't know anyone else was there when you threw a prescription bottle of pills in the trash. After you left, I looked at the bottle. The side effects caused fatigue and lethargic behavior. The medicine was for multiple personality disorder."

I let out a chuckle. Tanner had a good imagination. I'd give him that. I was curious as to where he was going with all this so I let him continue his rant.

"When Devin disappeared, I didn't think much of it. But when Les went missing, I started to put two and two together. You were suddenly the #1 receiver on the team. And you were no longer lethargic and lazy. You were fast. You were motivated. And you were mean. You were like a different person!"

I had enough of Tanner's nonsense.

"Shut up, Tanner!"

"I saw you hit Bud Bryant over the head with a baseball bat by his car and then you stuffed him in the trunk. You drove his car to the lake by your house and pushed it in."

Suddenly my head began to spin and I found myself on my hands and knees. I was bowled over by memories of choking Devin Brown to death and poisoning Les Tolbert's booze. I put their bodies in their cars, drove them to the lake by my house and pushed them in.

Tears were streaming down Tanner's face as he continued.

"I'm guilty. Guilty of not telling anybody. Hell, I was happy when Devin went missing. I always had a thing for his girl. With him out of the way, I was able to make a move on her. With Bud Bryant dead, I was the star running back."

Tanner's head drooped forward and I could see his shoulders shaking as he sobbed.

"I sit by that lake every day and contemplate whether or not I should tell somebody about what really happened, but I never do. Because I'm happy. Things are working out for me and I don't want anything to change. So, I may not have killed anyone, but I'm guilty too.

Tanner and I never said another word to each other ever again. And we never told anyone about our secret. We kept playing football and we both received football scholarships that we would never have gotten had we stayed buried on the bench.

Yes, I have a dark side, but I make a point to take a little bit of my medicine here and there. Enough to keep me from getting too mean. Enough to keep me from killing.

But I know deep down that if someone is standing in my way and keeping me from achieving a goal, it's very likely that I'll allow my dark side to take over again.

SERIAL KILLER ON THE LOOSE
The Witness

There's a serial killer on the loose. So far they have killed eight people all throughout Hopkins County, Kentucky. The killer uses the victim's blood to write a number next to the body indicating the kill count.

Upon examining multiple bodies, the coroner theorizes that the weapon being used is a six inch hunting knife with a jagged edge. Based on the entry wounds, detectives surmise that the killer is left handed.

The killer is clever and has never murdered in the same town more than once. They rarely leave any hint of a clue behind. Leads are scarce and thus far the detectives can only assume that the killer lives in or near Hopkins County, Kentucky. But anyone could have figured that much out.

Any potential trail leading to the killer had been virtually nonexistent. That is until recently, when the murderer seems to have gotten sloppy.

Victim number seven was found in the town of Dawson Springs. And then something unexpected happened. Victim number eight was also found in Dawson Springs.

My name is Claude Baron. I am the only witness to any of the murders. I saw the killer in the final stages of murdering victim number eight.

It was a Sunday night, well after midnight. Normally, I would have been asleep, but I got caught up in watching reruns of *The Brady Bunch* and lost track of time.

I thought I heard a muffled scream in the distance. Dawson Springs is a quiet town. No bars. No late night restaurants. Not many people out and about late, so I made a point to step out on my front porch to make sure everything seemed okay.

That's when I saw him.

Just a block down, toward the end of my street in a vacant lot, I saw a man stooping down. He was in the process of stabbing the victim. I yelled out, "Hey!" which made the killer stand up and look around. I couldn't see them very well, but they were on the short side and stocky. Definitely a man. After the killer ran away, I called the police.

The fact that the last two victims were killed in Dawson Springs had detectives deducting that the killer likely lived in Dawson Springs or very close by. It was the best lead they had since the murders began.

I held a neighborhood meeting at my house and dozens of people showed up. I suggested we start a neighborhood watch and it wasn't difficult to find volunteers.

A man named Will, opted to be the neighborhood watch leader and helped to create a patrolling schedule. Now we always have someone walking the streets at every hour of the night. The moment they see anything suspicious they'll alert all of the neighborhood watch participants and we'll converge.

If the killer attempts to strike in our town again, we'll be ready.

SERIAL KILLER ON THE LOOSE
The Copycat

My name is Reed. I live in Dawson Springs, Kentucky. And I am the serial killer on the loose.

Kinda.

The real killer started by making kills in the towns of Madisonville, Earlington, White Plains, Nebo, Nortonville and Hanson.

Then they stopped. Which was a bummer. I was a big fan of the killer. I wanted them to keep going. I enjoyed their work.

The killer had murdered one person every month. But for the last three months, crickets. Nothing.

What happened? Did they move? Did they die? Are they in jail somewhere? Maybe a mental institution?

Whatever the case, I assumed since that hadn't struck in three months that they had retired and I took it upon myself to grab the baton and continue the kill streak.

The killer hadn't christened my hometown of Dawson Springs yet, so I figured it was time to put it on the map. I started by killing an ex-girlfriend of mine. She was a real bitch. I told her when she broke up with me that I'd get even one day. I used a hunting knife, kind of like the one that they say the killer uses and I'm naturally left handed, so that worked out great.

I wanted my hometown to stand out, so I decided to make it the first town to receive two murders. My second victim was my boss. He was a jerk. He threatened to fire me if I showed up for work late one more time.

Someone spotted me as I was doing the killing. Luckily, I still had time to smear the bloody kill count number by my boss's head before I ran away.

When it dawned on me that the two people who I killed could be traced back to me, I thought it was important to try to do a few things to throw any pesky investigators off my trail.

The first thing I did was join the neighborhood watch. Nobody would suspect one of the neighborhood watch volunteers as being the killer, would they?

Next, I'd kill a third person. A random person. Someone I didn't know. I honed in a woman who worked at one of the stores in town. She was new to the area. I had no ties to her whatsoever, so she would be my next victim.

I spent a little time stalking her. Waiting for the perfect moment. When she went for a stroll down a quiet street after dark, I made my move. I started inching closer to her and withdrew my knife. That's when I heard a man's voice behind me.

"Stop right there."

I turned around. It was Will, the neighborhood watch leader. He motioned to the weapon in my hand.

"Nice knife."

"Oh yeah. Well, I'm patrolling the streets. I figured a weapon would be handy."

"It's not your night to patrol."

"It's not? Huh. I must have gotten my dates confused."

Will had cold, dark brown eyes. They were almost black. His stare was intimidating as was his frame. He was a tall, athletic man. Much bigger than me. I sure wouldn't want to tangle with him.

"You were going to kill her weren't you?"

I instinctively looked back in the direction of the girl I was stalking, who was now long gone. I used that as an opportunity to play dumb.

"What girl? I don't see anybody."

Will stepped closer to me. He held a snarl as he spoke.

"I know you're the killer."

Will sure seemed convinced. I let out a deep breath and shrugged. I was caught. At least I'd get credit for doing all eight of the murders and not just the last two. Hell, I'd be famous.

"Okay fine. You caught me. I'm the killer. I killed them all. Take me in."

I watched as Will removed something from under his coat. I assumed it was handcuffs or some other kind of restraint. I was a little surprised to see that it was a knife. A big knife with a jagged edge and he was holding it in his left hand. I was even more surprised when he raised the knife high into the air.

SERIAL KILLER ON THE LOOSE
Neighborhood Watch Leader

My name is Will. I live in Dawson Springs, Kentucky. And I am the serial killer on the loose.

I take meticulous measures to make sure that am never caught. I never kill anyone that authorities can trace back to me. I wear latex gloves as to never leave fingerprints. I only kill when there are no signs of witnesses anywhere in the vicinity. Even though I'm naturally right handed, I stab with my left hand, to throw detectives off. And most importantly, I absolutely never ever kill in my hometown of Dawson Springs.

I had been on quite a roll with my murders. I had killed six people in six months in six different towns. Nobody had any clue that it was me and I had no plans of stopping anytime soon. But I also didn't want to follow any discernable patterns for any length of time. That's the reason I decided to take some time off from killing. The plan was four or five months of quiet before I started up again.

To say I was angry when some half-wit copycat started taking credit for my kills was an understatement. And worse yet, he was killing in my hometown.

Unacceptable!

When a witness to one of his murders formed a neighborhood watch, I was quick to take the reins. That way I'd have access to every member and their watch schedule.

The copycat killer would almost definitely join the neighborhood watch as a diversion. From there it was just a matter of matching up the copycat's two victims to the neighborhood watch participants. It took me no time at all to figure out it was Reed.

After I killed Reed, I wrote the number seven next to him in his own blood.

At first, investigators would be baffled as to why the number had been repeated. Once I killed my next victim, in a different town and put the number eight next to them, they'd start to figure it out. Eventually, they'd link Reed's murders back to him and expunge his clumsy murders from my record.

In the future, I'll add another telltale sign to my victims to prove that they're mine. Maybe I'll cut off a finger or an ear or carve something into their flesh.

I'll think of something.

Hopefully the detectives will wise up and not share that information with the press in order to prevent further pathetic copy cats such as Reed.

THE STRANGE TALE OF FLIGHT 636

I've lived in Chicago all my life. If you don't know much about Chicago, the winters can be brutal. After thirty six years, I was ready for a change so when I had the opportunity to interview for a job in Orlando, Florida, I jumped at the chance. I was eager to trade in the cold Chicago winters for the hot Orlando summers!

It was a Tuesday afternoon. I had booked a flight that would get me into Orlando the day before the interview. This would allow me to settle in at my hotel, have a nice, relaxing dinner and get a good night's sleep. I would most assuredly be well rested for my interview the following morning.

I got to the airport early enough to have a drink and a snack at the airport bar before I boarded my flight. As I sat in the corner of the bar sipping a glass of bourbon and munching on some fried cheese sticks, I spent some time taking in one of my favorite time killing activities. People watching.

I immediately took note of a man sitting at the end of the bar. He had puffy black hair and a prominent handlebar mustache. He was wearing a loud Hawaiian shirt and red plaid pants. As much as his appearance stood out, what really caught my eye was the way he was drinking.

The eccentric man had the bartender line up five shots on the bar. Each shot glass contained a different form of alcohol. If I heard correctly the shots consisted of rum, whiskey, tequila, vodka and gin. The mustached man then proceeded to wolf down each shot one immediately after the other. He followed the alcoholic intake with a theatrical full body shiver. From there he threw some cash at the bartender and waltzed out of the bar.

I was the very first person to board the plane. I took my seat which was located in the middle of the plane on the aisle. I usually have to use the restroom at least one time per flight and hate having to climb over people, so I always make a point to book an aisle seat.

When I heard muffled laughter coming from the back of the plane, I was a little bit surprised. I was the first one on. I didn't notice anyone at the back of the plane when I boarded. When I turned to find the source of the laughter, I assumed I'd see a flight attendant in the back of the plane performing some kind of preflight duty. To my surprise I didn't see anyone. No flight attendant. No other passengers. Nobody.

It was then that other passengers began entering the plane and I shifted my attention from the odd occurrence to checking out my fellow airline passengers.

I immediately took note of the woman carrying an infant. Oh, how I hoped she wasn't sitting anywhere near me! Luckily she took a seat toward the front of the plane.

Next I noticed an extremely attractive woman with exciting, bright blue eyes. She was within my age range. Whether she was single or not wasn't relevant because I wasn't brash enough to attempt to pick up a stranger on a plane. Still, I wouldn't have minded her sitting next to me. She didn't however, instead choosing a seat a few rows behind me.

I let out a chuckle when I saw the next passenger boarding. It was the gaudy dressed man with the distinct handlebar mustache. Not surprisingly, he was subtly staggering as he meandered down the aisle. I noticed that he took a seat all the way at the back of the plane.

After all of the people had boarded and taken their seats, my people watching options became scarce so I decided to begin settling in for the flight.

I like to pass time in a plane by reading. I like horror books, preferably horror anthologies that have a collection of several short scary stories. The book I picked for this flight was called *Blood Tingling Tales*. I decided to start reading while the flight crew prepared for takeoff. I was only a few pages in when I heard a ruckus coming from the back of the plane.

At first I just heard a man ranting about something. Much of what he was saying was a garbled mess and I couldn't make it out, but I distinctly heard him say "I want to get off this plane! Let me off this plane, now!"

Every passenger on the plane turned around to see what the commotion was about, including me. I wasn't sure if I should have been surprised or not when I recognized that the person at the center of the hubbub was none other than the handlebar mustached man. He was speaking seriously to one of the flight attendants.

"Stop this plane. I want off! I want to get off this plane right now!"

The flight attendant kept cool and calm as she explained to the hysterical man that the flight was returning to the gate to let him off. She was valiantly attempting to keep the man calm and was asking him if he had any carry-on luggage to take with him.

"I don't care about my luggage. Just let me off this plane!"

When the plane finally got back to the gate, the intoxicated man hurried down the aisle toward the cabin door and he shouted out a drunken slurred warning to the rest of the passengers on the flight.

"I'm getting off of this plane right now. You should all get off of it too. If you don't you're going to die!"

Just before exiting the plane the man stopped and addressed all of us one more time.

"You all need to get off this plane! I don't care if you believe me or not! You can get off this plane with me and live or you can stay here and die."

The man then pointed toward the back of the plane.

"That son of a bitch back there is a ghost!"

With that, he departed.

My fellow passengers started looking around at each other in disbelief. Some began laughing and within seconds the plane was abuzz at the outrageous scene we had all just witnessed.

This was undoubtedly going to delay takeoff so I decided to take that opportunity to empty my bladder. While I was in the restroom, I could hear the rumbled chatter within the plane dying down as people transitioned back to their pre-flight rituals.

Upon exiting the restroom, I made a motion to head back to my seat when I did a double-take as I noticed a man standing in the far back corner of the plane with his eyes closed. He was unusually thin and his skin was taut and appeared grayish in color. I jumped when he opened his eyes. They were solid white. No color. No pupil, just solid white eyes. And then he smiled the creepiest of smiles. It was an abnormally wide smile that seemed to take up the majority of his face. That's when he let forth with a hideous malevolent laugh.

Suddenly the room began to spin. I closed my eyes tight to combat the dizziness. The evil laughter echoed through my mind as I saw a vision of an airplane exploding in the sky.

"I'm going to kill all of you!"

I snapped my eyes open when I heard the demonic voice in front of my face, but everything was back to normal. The spinning sensation had vanished. The ghostly man in the corner was gone. The evil laughter was overtaken by the murmurs of passengers chattering away.

It was then that I realized that the handlebar mustached man must have experienced something similar to me. He wasn't just a raving, drunken lunatic. He saw the vision. He knew as I now did that this flight was doomed!

"Everybody get off this plane! It's going to explode!"

I hurried down the aisle shaking people and warning them.

"There's a ghost on this plane! This plane is going to blow up! It's going to crash the plane!"

Nobody was taking me seriously. They all thought I was nuts. Multiple people had taken out their phones and were recording my frantic warnings.

"I'm not crazy! I'm not drunk! I just saw a ghost at the back of the plane! It's going to kill us all!"

I wasn't going to voluntarily leave. I had to do something or every person on that plane was going to die!

Eventually a troop of security and police officers arrived and physically carried me off the plane as I continued to shout and warn everyone about the premonition I had.

I was arrested and booked for disorderly conduct.

My understanding is that the flight was delayed by three hours during which time they did a thorough search of the entire plane before finally deeming it safe to fly.

The airplane exploded and crashed twenty minutes after takeoff.

There were no survivors.

THE VIAL

I work for a small, independently owned clothing retailer in Nashville TN. Most days it's a three person operation. My boss, Judy, is there every day we're open and is normally accompanied by two saleswomen.

On the day in question the saleswomen were me and a younger gal named Tracy. Tracy was fresh out of college, but had learned the ropes quickly.

I always had lunch at a small diner down the street. I ordered the same thing every day, a grilled cheese and fries. I ate there often enough that I could simply say "the usual" when I was asked what I wanted.

I was sitting at the counter chitchatting with the waitress when the commotion began. The first thing we noticed was the sirens. At first we didn't think anything of it. It was a big city. Occasional sirens were the norm. But on this day there were a lot of them. There must have been a dozen police cars nearing the restaurant and everyone in the establishment took notice.

The harsh sound of screeching tires was followed by a loud crash on the street in front of the diner. Everyone rushed outside to see what happened. The entrance to the restaurant was so jam packed with patrons rubbernecking to witness the cause of the crash, that I wasn't going to be able to see anything that way.

In the back of the diner near the kitchen was an exit that the employees used. It led to an alley. I hurried out the exit and had a great view of the disorder.

There was a small car that was wrapped around a traffic light. They must have lost control of their vehicle. The driver's side door of the vehicle was ajar and I didn't see anyone inside.

A fleet of police cars grinded to a halt and cries of "stop" and "freeze" filled the air. I couldn't see who they were shouting at, but what I did notice was that it wasn't just the police in pursuit. I saw military jeeps and cargo trucks.

My focus was so dialed in on the vehicles, that I hadn't even noticed the man before he barreled into me. He had gray hair and was wearing a white lab coat. His head had a nasty gash that was bleeding profusely. He was huffing and puffing and when I noticed how frenzied he was, I finally realized he was the driver of the crashed vehicle. This was the apparent fugitive they were after!

Before I could even contemplate how to properly react, the distraught man pushed a small vial into my hand. It was the size of a nail polish bottle and held some kind of dark brown liquid.

"This will destroy the world! Get rid of it!"

In his hysterical state, the man pushed the vial against me so hard that the corked top popped off and the contents spilled out all over my hands. When the man noticed this, his eyes opened wide and filled with fear.

"Oh no! Oh my God, no!"

The frantic man held his fear filled gaze on me for a moment before he turned and dashed into the street. He was instantly met with an array of bullets that thudded into his chest and dropped him to the ground.

My scream of terror blended in with the rest of the cries from horrified onlookers, but I didn't run away. I couldn't. I was frozen with fright and witnessed two men in army fatigues desperately searching through the dead man's lab coat. The longer they searched, the more panicked they became.

"I can't find it! It's not here!"

They began scanning the area urgently.

"He must have given it to somebody!"

It was the vial! They were looking for the vial.

I could see them looking in my direction, which made sense, that was the direction from which the dead man had come.

What should I do?

My first instinct was to tell the military people what happened. But they were so quick to kill the man in the lab coat, would they kill me too if they knew I had come in contact with the vial?

I hurried back into the restaurant. I snuck a quick peek over my shoulder just before the door closed behind me and could see multiple men in army fatigues rushing my way.

Did they see me? I wasn't sure. But if they came into the diner and spotted me running, they'd probably shoot first and ask questions later!

I noticed that the kitchen to the diner was empty. The employees were still out front watching the drama, so I stepped into the kitchen and quickly tied on an apron to give the appearance that I belonged there. Just as I picked up a spatula, the exit door flew open and two military men entered.

The men were flustered and appeared worried. They quickly gazed around the diner before affixing their stare on me.

"Did you see anyone come through here?"

I shook my head.

"No. Nobody."

The men took my statement at face value and dashed back outside.

"They must have gone down the alley! Hurry!"

I could hear dozens of footsteps clomping by the door. I waited until I couldn't hear them anymore before I took the apron off and left through the entrance of the diner.

I felt like a football player as I darted through the hordes of onlookers who were trying to ascertain what was going on. I didn't feel safe until I got back to the store.

Judy and Tracy were both standing outside, when I arrived. The store was too far away for them to have seen anything, but they heard enough to know it was something serious.

Judy immediately noticed that I was distressed.

"Are you okay, dear?"

I took in a few deep breaths as I attempted to collect myself.

"Yes, yes…I'm fine. I'll be okay."

Tracy seemed less concerned with my condition and more interested in what had happened.

"What's all the commotion about? Did you see anything?"

There was no way I was going to confide in them. I figured the less people who knew about my contact with the vial, the better.

"No, I didn't see much. I think there was a car crash."

Tracy wasn't satisfied.

"We heard gunshots!"

I shrugged.

"I don't know."

That's when I realized that my hands were burning. They felt like they were on fire!

I let out a shriek of pain as I rushed into the store and into the bathroom. I immediately stuck my hands under the faucet and let cold water flow over them.

I didn't have time to be concerned with the fact that the cold water wasn't helping in the slightest because I broke out in an uncontrollable coughing fit.

I leaned over the sink when I felt the vomit rising up in my throat and a burst of bright red blood exploded from my mouth along with thick chunks of tissue.

Then I noticed my hands. They were rotting away in front of my eyes. My flesh was disintegrating and turning into thick, warm, sticky pus. The stench of decay filled the air as I watched my flesh, which now looked like liquefied ground beef, drip off of my hands and splat onto the sink in front of me.

I was horror-struck when I caught my reflection in the mirror. The pale skin of my face looked like rawhide. It had grown taut, accentuating the outline of my skull. My eyes had frosted over white. My pupils were gone. My hair was thinning. I ran my bony fingers through it and it came out in clumps along with bacon-like strips from my scalp.

My entire body felt as though it was engulfed in flames and I would have expected to be hyperventilating at that point, but I wasn't. As a matter of fact, I wasn't breathing at all. My chest wasn't moving. I wasn't drawing breath. I held my skeletal hand to my heart and felt nothing.

What was happening to me?

I heard a knock at the door, followed by its opening. Judy popped her head in.

"Are you okay dear?"

When she saw the grotesque thing I had become she opened her mouth to scream, but only a wheeze of disgust emerged.

I'm not sure exactly why, but I wanted to kill Judy. More than that, I wanted to eat her. I charged her, knocked her to the ground and ripped a jagged hunk of meat from her forearm.

Tracy made the mistake of rushing to Judy's aid. The second she came into my view, I tackled her and sank my teeth into her. Crimson gushed from the wound as I tore stringy strands of flesh from Tracy's throat.

I never tasted anything so succulent in my life and more importantly, it momentarily stopped the scorching pain that had overtaken my body.

I looked up when I saw Judy step toward me. Her skin seemed to be melting off her body like hot, gooey ice cream. I watched as she lethargically meandered outside and took a bite out of the first person who was unfortunate enough to pass by.

The second mouthful I ripped from Tracy's body wasn't as tasty, nor did it ease the burning pain as well as the first bite did. I needed to find someone new to feed on and luckily, there were plenty outside.

Before I could even reach the door, a disgustingly decomposing Tracy had risen up and pushed me out of the way. She needed to feed too.

The competition was fierce, but luckily there were throngs of people to chomp down on. The problem was that each person that we took a bite of rapidly transitioned into the rotten, putrid, oozing beings that we had become.

I sank my teeth into as many people as I could, but within hours everyone I saw was just like me. The source to suppress our blistering pain was quickly becoming scarce, but we'd never stop searching for more.

Never.

I THINK I KILLED SOMEBODY LAST NIGHT

I woke up in my bed with my skull throbbing. I felt like I had been hit in the head with a brick. It took me a few minutes to open my eyes and then a few more minutes before I finally rose up.

When I gazed down at my hands, I was shocked.

"What the hell?"

My knuckles were bloody and my hands were covered in dirt. And I don't just mean dirty, I mean they were caked in what appeared to be topsoil. I turned my hands over to see that both of my palms were blistered.

I got out of bed, stumbled into the bathroom and was in for another surprise when I looked in the mirror and saw the state of my face. I had a fat lip, a bruise under my left eye and scratches on my neck.

"What the hell happened?"

That was a good question and one I could not answer.

I rested my head in my hands as I tried to remember something, anything, from the previous night.

I live a simple life. I work a 9 to 5 construction job Monday through Friday. I have salad for dinner almost every night and on Friday nights I go to a local pub and drink the night away.

That's the way the previous night started. I got off work, went to the pub had their Santa Fe salad and started drinking. Shortly after that, I remember absolutely nothing.

I took a shower, got dressed and stepped out on my porch. My neighbor, Adam, was doing some yard work. He spotted me and gave me a courtesy wave and shout.

"Hi, Mark!"

I smiled and waved back. As I bent down to pick up the day's paper, I noticed a yellow cab dropping off someone down the road. After they dropped them off, they slowly pulled up to my house and stopped.

"You look a hell of a lot better than you did last night!"

I furrowed my brow in confusion as I walked up to the cab.

"You saw me last night?"

The cab driver was an older man with sole patch and wearing a fedora.

"Yeah. I brought you home."

"Where did I come from?"

"A little house over on Barbary Street."

"Barbary Street?"

I didn't know anyone on Barbary Street. And I never went to that neighborhood. It was way on the other side of town.

Why was I there last night?

I had to find out so I hopped into the cab.

"Take me to where you picked me up."

As the cabbie drove, I leaned over the seat so he could hear my question well.

"Was I bloody and covered in dirt last night?"

He nodded.

"Do you know how I got that way?"

He shook his head.

"You mean I was all covered in dirt and blood when you picked me up and you didn't ask me what happened?"

He shrugged.

"I get paid to drive folks to and from. Not to ask questions."

The cab driver pulled up to a small, powder blue, ranch style house. I had no recollection of the house, whatsoever. I verified with the cabbie that this was the correct address and he insisted that it was.

After I paid the cabbie and he departed, I stood in front of the house for a few minutes trying to remember something. Nothing was ringing a bell, so I walked up to the front door and knocked.

There was no answer.

I knocked several more times and got no response. I looked around the quiet neighborhood and didn't' see anyone, so I opted to try turning the doorknob. To my surprise the door was unlocked.

I was curious enough about what happened to me the previous night to slowly open the front door to the house and pop my head in.

"Hello? Anyone home?"

There was no answer, so I stepped inside.

The interior of the house was nothing special, but very tidy. I walked through the small house in hopes that something would jog my memory, but I couldn't remember a damn thing.

I figured I should vacate the premises before someone spotted me prowling around and called the police. As I opened the door, I was met by a short, pudgy woman with light brown hair.

"Are you a friend of Vanessa?"

I put up a confident front to make it seem like I belonged there.

"Yep. I'm a good friend of hers."

"Were you the one digging in her back yard last night?"

"Digging?"

The neighbor nodded.

"I heard a noise last night at about 3:00am. I looked out the back window and could see a man in her backyard digging a hole or something. I thought that was strange so I wanted to come by today and make sure everything was okay."

"Oh yeah. Everything's fine. Thanks for checking."

The woman held a suspicious gaze on me for a moment before finally walking away. Once she was gone, I quickly went back inside and rushed to the backyard.

I saw the shovel stuck in the ground next to a mound of churned soil. It took me a few seconds to realize that it had the appearance of a freshly covered grave.

I looked down at my blistered hands.

Did I dig that grave? And if so why?

Did I…kill someone?

I had to get out of the house. If I did murder someone and bury them in the backyard, it probably wasn't wise to be hanging around. As I started to exit the house, I noticed a red book of matches sitting on a table by the front door. The matchbook read "The Rabbit in Red Lounge."

I knew the place. It was just a few doors down from the pub that I frequented. It was a highfalutin establishment that served drinks that were way too expensive.

At this point I should have been planning a getaway, but I was too baffled and curious to skip town without finding out some answers, so I decided to stop at The Rabbit in Red Lounge.

The establishment was on the small side and draped in red velvet. I sat at the bar and ordered a club soda and chopped salad. The salad was decent, but not worth the steep price they charged.

When I finished the salad I made a little small talk with the bartender before I slid out a casual question.

"Hey, do you know a girl who comes here named, Vanessa?"

"Yeah, she works here. Was supposed to show up for work an hour ago. I tried calling but got no answer. Probably hung over."

"Why do you say that?"

"She was here last night for a drink. She was already drunk off her ass. She was bar hopping."

"Was she with anyone?"

"No. But she did say some creepy guy was following her."

"Creepy guy? Do you know who?"

He shook his head.

"When did she leave?"

"I don't know. 9:30pm. 10:00pm, maybe. If you see her, tell her to call me and let me know why she's late."

I gave the bartender a nice tip and then got up and left.

Was the creepy guy that was following her, me?

I decided to stop by the pub that I frequented. As I stepped into the pub, I noticed my buddy, Slim, sitting at the bar. When he spotted me his eyes widened. He rushed to my side and spoke in a discreet whisper.

"What the hell man? What did you do last night?"

"What? What do you mean?"

"I saw you chasing a woman down the street."

"Me? Are you sure?"

"Of course I'm sure! It was two in the morning. I was leaving the pub here and I saw her come running out of the alley and down the street screaming. She only had one shoe on. And her hair was all messed up. And *you* were chasing her!"

Slim recognized the confused expression on my face.

"You don't remember."

"Slim, I don't remember anything last night!"

"I'm not surprised. You showed up right after work and drank me under the table. How many times have I told you that you need to eat more than just a salad before you start drinking?"

"Do you remember when I left here?"

"It was around 9:30pm or 10:00pm."

"That early?"

"Yeah, you saw a real pretty blond walk by outside and said you were going to go talk to her. Come to think of it, that was the girl you were chasing!"

I dropped my head into my hands.

"Mark, I hope you didn't do anything stupid."

"Yeah. Me too."

I wasn't sure where to go from there, so I headed home. As I walked toward my front door, I was approached by my next door neighbor, Adam.

"Hey Mark, the police were just here looking for you."

My heart sank.

"For me? What did they want?"

"They didn't say. You're not in any trouble are you?"

"I hope not."

I sat in my living room thinking everything through. Based on all the evidence it sure sounded like I killed that woman and buried the body in her backyard. I was contemplating whether or not to turn myself in or make a run for it. But ultimately, I decided I was going to have to be one hundred percent certain before I made a decision. I had to go back to the woman's house, dig up the grave and see for myself.

I wasted no time once I got to the house. I rushed into the backyard, pulled the shovel out of the ground and began uncovering the grave. The dirt was so soft it would only take a few minutes before I uncovered her dead face…

"Mark?"

I jumped and even let out a yelp when I heard the feminine voice. I looked up to see an extremely attractive blonde with the most heavenly blue eyes I had ever seen.

"Vanessa?"

"I woke up and you were gone. Kind of a crazy night, huh?"

I took in a few breaths. Did this mean I didn't kill anyone?

"To be honest, I don't remember much about last night. I was hoping you could clue me in on some of the details."

"Sure. Which details?"

"All of them?"

She laughed.

"I was bar hopping around town like I do every Friday night. Everywhere I went, I noticed a big, creepy guy staring at me."

"Big, creepy guy? You mean, it wasn't me?"

"You? No! You saw me walking down the road and started chitchatting with me. That's when I noticed the creepy guy standing in the alleyway, staring at me. I pointed him out and you confronted him."

"I did?"

"Yes. It was very brave of you, but the guy went crazy and attacked you. He was a lot bigger than you. He was working you over pretty good and had you down on the ground, so I ran over, took off one of my shoes and hit him over the head with it. He let you go, grabbed me by the hair and started shaking me around. That's when you got back up, spun him around and knocked him out cold with one punch!"

I looked down at my bloody knuckles.

"Really?"

"I freaked out and went running down the street. You caught up to me and together we found a police officer and told him what happened. Turns out, the man was an escaped mental patient they had been looking for."

"You're kidding?"

"Nope. The policeman said he was going to come to your house and present you with some kind of citizen award for helping to catch the crazy guy."

"That explains why they were looking for me. What happened after that?"

"We came back to my place."

"Oh, really?"

She gave me a playful slap on the shoulder.

"No, not for that! Somehow the subject of salad came up."

"I'm not surprised. I love salad."

"And I make the best Greek salad in the world. But you seemed skeptical so I brought you back home to make you a salad. When we got here, I saw that I didn't have any vegetables and I guess I started ranting about how I needed to plant my own garden. And sweetheart that you are, you went out back and started digging up the ground! It was shortly after that, when I passed out. I woke up this morning and you were gone. But the ground is ready for me to plant a garden! So thank you for that!"

I shook my head in disbelief.

"That was the most fantastic story I have ever heard. It's a shame I can't remember any of it. I guess I should stop drinking so much."

"You and me both."

We shared a light chuckle and then sat quietly for a long moment before Vanessa finally broke the silence.

"Mark?"

"Yes."

"Let's keep the crazy story going. How about a nice, peaceful dinner tonight?"

I smiled.

"It's a date."

STRANDED AFTER THE CRASH
The Passenger

My name is Wyatt. I'm a survivor of a commercial plane crash.

The plane crashed into the ocean. Those who died upon impact were the lucky ones. The rest drowned in the depths of the cold, black water.

I would have drowned too if I didn't see a seat cushion floating by me just as I was about to sink from exhaustion. I grabbed the floatation device and passed out. I found myself washed up on the shore of a deserted island the following day.

The island is small and while there are an abundance of trees, none of them bear fruit or coconuts.

Food is scarce. If I can't catch fish from the ocean, I go hungry.

There is a tiny stream near the forest's edge. It's drinkable if I boil it, but if there's no rain for a few days, it dries up.

I can't remember exactly how long I've been here. Forty days. Fifty days, maybe.

There was only one other survivor. The pilot of the plane. His name is Blake. He's not the best companion to be stranded with. As a matter of fact it's very much like being alone, except I have to split my food and water.

Blake spends most of his time down the beach away from me. I think he plummeted into a deep depression knowing that he was piloting the plane that crashed and killed over two hundred people.

When he does interact with me, he's short and to the point. I used to check on him during the first few weeks. But one can only hear the words "leave me alone" so often before they begin to take heed of the request.

I sleep in a small cave near the ocean's edge. On stormy nights, Blake joins me. Otherwise, he sleeps on the beach.

If I catch any fish, I place half of them near the area Blake spends most of his time. He has never done the same for me. Either he's not trying to catch fish or he's not sharing.

Sometimes I consider moving to the back end of the island to be away from Blake and we can just live solitary lives and fend for ourselves. But if it's me that's keeping Blake alive, that would kill him. I couldn't do that. So, I do my part to help us both survive.

Once I suggested that we work together to build an SOS fire, but Blake insisted it was a waste of time and energy. Still, I gathered together a large pile of kindling to light if I ever hear a plane nearby. I also used rocks and twigs to create the letters SOS that could be seen from the air.

I'm trying. Without any help from Blake.

We've reached the most desperate of times on the island. I hadn't been able to catch any fish for days and the recent lack of rain had dried up our water source. With the conditions as they were, I knew our time was running out.

It was a warm, still night when I heard the sound. It was distant.

At first I thought it could be the hum of a plane or the blare of a boat's horn. When I heard the sound again and again and again in rhythmic beats, I realized what it was.

The deep bellow of a bongo drum.

I rushed out of my cave and looked around. I thought maybe it was something Blake was doing, but it was clear that the bongo drums were coming from a great distance away.

From the other side of the island.

I instantly rushed into the dense island jungle toward the sound of the drums. I quickly succumbed to exhaustion as my body was significantly malnourished at that point. I fell to my knees and sucked in as much breath as I could.

After a few deep inhales, my adrenaline kicked in and began flowing through my body. It gave me enough strength to charge forward through the jungle.

The drums were getting louder. I was getting closer. Salvation was upon me!

When the drums abruptly stopped all hope was lost for a fleeting moment. That's when I saw a scrolled up piece of parchment lying next to a small, primitive shovel that was sticking in the ground.

I rushed to the scroll and unrolled it. The message was scribbled hastily in ink.

Use the shovel to dig three feet into the earth.
There you will find a hatch.
Open it.

Inside the hatch is enough food and water for one person to live on, for ninety days.
On the ninetieth day a boat will arrive on the island and you will be rescued.

The message was no more unbelievable than finding the scroll and shovel in the first place, so I started digging. Within minutes I found a thick, metal hatch with a large wheel latch. It took a fair amount of elbow grease, but I was able to turn the wheel. It squeaked in rusted defiance until the latch unfastened and I pulled the hatch open.

The message on the scroll was correct. There was a virtual stockpile of canned goods and bottled water. I raced down the ladder into the crude, underground shelter, ripped the top off of a can of tomatoes and swallowed them down. I followed that up by chugging two bottles of water. I cried tears of joy as my body absorbed the much needed nutrients.

After a moment of rest, I hurried back up the ladder. I had to tell Blake about the discovery. We had enough food and water to last us forty five days. Then all we had to do was find a way to last another forty five days and we'd be saved!

STRANDED AFTER THE CRASH
The Pilot

My name is Blake. I am the pilot of the plane that crashed.

And I crashed it intentionally.

I have a gambling problem and gambled away my life savings away. And not just mine, but my wife's too. And my son's college fund.

When my wife found out about my discrepancy she divorced me and took my son with her.

I had nothing and wanted to end it all. What easier way than to crash the commercial airliner into the ocean? Sure it would kill everyone else on board too, but I didn't care. I needed to die and this is how I knew to do it.

It took surviving the crash for me to realize I didn't want to die after all. If I did, I would have rolled off the piece of the wing I woke up floating on and dropped down to the bottom of the ocean.

But I wanted to live!

To my chagrin, I wasn't the only survivor. A passenger named Wyatt survived as well. This was bad news as he would take up much needed resources on the island.

I stayed away from Wyatt as much as possible. I fished in secret and ate everything I caught. I also hoarded as much water from our miniscule stream as I could.

I found out quickly that I wasn't a very good fisherman, but it turned out Wyatt was sharing half of his catches with me and that helped to keep me alive.

Sucker.

It was a warm, still night. I found myself lying on the beach staring up at the stars when I heard the drums. They were coming from the other side of the island.

We had been on the island for some time and this was the first sign of human life I had heard. Whoever it was surely would have food and water and a way to take me off of this God forsaken island!

I followed the sound until I found myself staring at three different items in the middle of the jungle. A scrolled up piece of paper, a shovel and a revolver.

I had just finished reading the scroll when I heard Wyatt tearing through the jungle toward me. I picked up the gun and hid in the shadows.

Wyatt read the scroll and helped me out by digging up the ground and opening the hatch. The smile held on his face when he emerged from the ground confirmed the validity of the scroll.

I'd have enough food and water to survive ninety days. Then I'd be rescued. Once I got back home, I'd likely get some settlement money from the airline and after double or tripling that money with some bets, I could be set for life!

Of course, there was the problem of Wyatt who was actually excited when he saw me.

"Blake, you're not going to believe what I just found!"

The damned fool didn't even notice I was pointing a gun at him.

The first shot seemed to surprise him. The second shot dropped him to the ground. I put the final bullet in the back of his head and that was the end of Wyatt.

STRANDED AFTER THE CRASH
The Island

I am the island.

Many people are sent to me after they die. I help to decide whether they are candidates for moving forward or going elsewhere.

In this case, Wyatt passed the test with flying colors while Blake failed miserably.

Two hundred and seventeen people died in the plane crash that day.

Wyatt and Blake were just two of them.

Two down. Two hundred and fifteen to go.

THE END

Chunks of Terror Vol. 2
Coming Soon

FINAL WORD

"Hudgins is a Horror-Meister to reckon with!"
VICTOR MILLER – *Writer of Friday the 13th*

I hope you enjoyed *Chunks of Terror Vol. 1.*
I'm dying for you to read *Volume 2* which will be available soon. Very soon.

In the meantime, if you haven't read my other horror anthology series yet, I highly recommend you do.

FRAGMENTS OF FRIGHT

You can grab the entire *Fragments of Fright* collection at the link below. All 5 Volumes bundled together into one huge boxed set!
https://www.amazon.com/dp/B0CM1GGVRR

Or if you prefer to go Volume to Volume, you can find all of them here:
https://www.amazon.com/dp/B0C3Z1RB7J

BLOOD TINGLING TALES

You can get the entire Blo*od Tingling Tales* collection at the link below. All 5 Volumes bundled together into one convenient boxed set!

https://www.amazon.com/gp/product/B0BWVJZB2T

Or if you prefer to go Volume to Volume, you can find all of them here:
https://www.amazon.com/dp/B0BK43LJNF

HORROR QUICKIES

Before *Chunks of Terror, Fragments of Fright* and *Blood Tingling Tales* there was *Horror Quickies*! The entire collection of 5 Volumes can be found at the following link:
https://www.amazon.com/dp/B0BC4WTPD6

Or if you prefer to read one Volume at a time, you can find all the individual Volumes here:
https://www.amazon.com/dp/B09WK689P8

FROM THE MIND OF A MANIAC

One other book I like to make sure people are aware of is called *From the Mind of a Maniac.*
I bundled all 8 of my stand alone books into one gigantic boxed set. All 8 stories are interconnected in some way. I think it's a lot of fun. You can get *From the Mind of a Maniac* here:
https://www.amazon.com/dp/B0BZLXJ9R8

ACKNOWLEDGEMENTS

A big thank you to my wonderful advanced reader team A.K.A. *The Super Maniacs* and to Doreen and Sherie for helping me weed out the typos!
Thanks to Naomi for her terrifyingly awesome cover work!
And of course a huge thank you to every one of my maniacal fans out there in the world, wherever you are!

WHERE TO FIND ME

To keep up on my latest books you can visit my Amazon Author Page where all of my books are listed by popularity:
https://www.amazon.com/stores/Steve-Hudgins/author/B07KH2GMBF

Or you can visit the book section of my website which will show a list of my books from newest to oldest:
https://www.maniacontheloose.com/books

You can find all the audiobooks I have available here:
https://www.maniacontheloose.com/audiobooks

While you're at my website, be sure to sign up for my newsletter. You'll get access to some free stuff and be kept up to date on all the latest crazy things I have going on! Or sign up now:
https://subscribepage.io/maniac

At my website you may notice a PODCAST button. There you will find my podcast, *Maniac on the Loose Scary Stories*. It's where I read some of my short horror stories accompanied by creepy background music! I release new episodes every week.
Here's the link to that:
https://www.maniacontheloose.com/podcasts

Another section of my website that you may spot is the MOVIES section.
At one time I was making no-budget feature length indie horror films. If you want to check any of those out you can just follow this link

to find out what streaming outlets they are available on, but keep in mind these were all made with no budget and it shows: https://www.maniacontheloose.com/bigbitingpigproductions

If you want to follow me on any social media places this is where you can find me!

Goodreads:
https://www.goodreads.com/author/show/18624636.Steve_Hudgins
Bookbub:
https://www.bookbub.com/profile/steve-hudgins
Facebook:
https://www.facebook.com/SteveHudginsWriter
Twitter/X:
https://twitter.com/BigBitingPig

I hope *Chunks of Terror Vol. 1* brought you some terrifying fun.
There's more on the way!

www.maniacontheloose.com